COLOR THE CLASSICS:

Beauty & the Beast

A Deeply Romantic Coloring Book

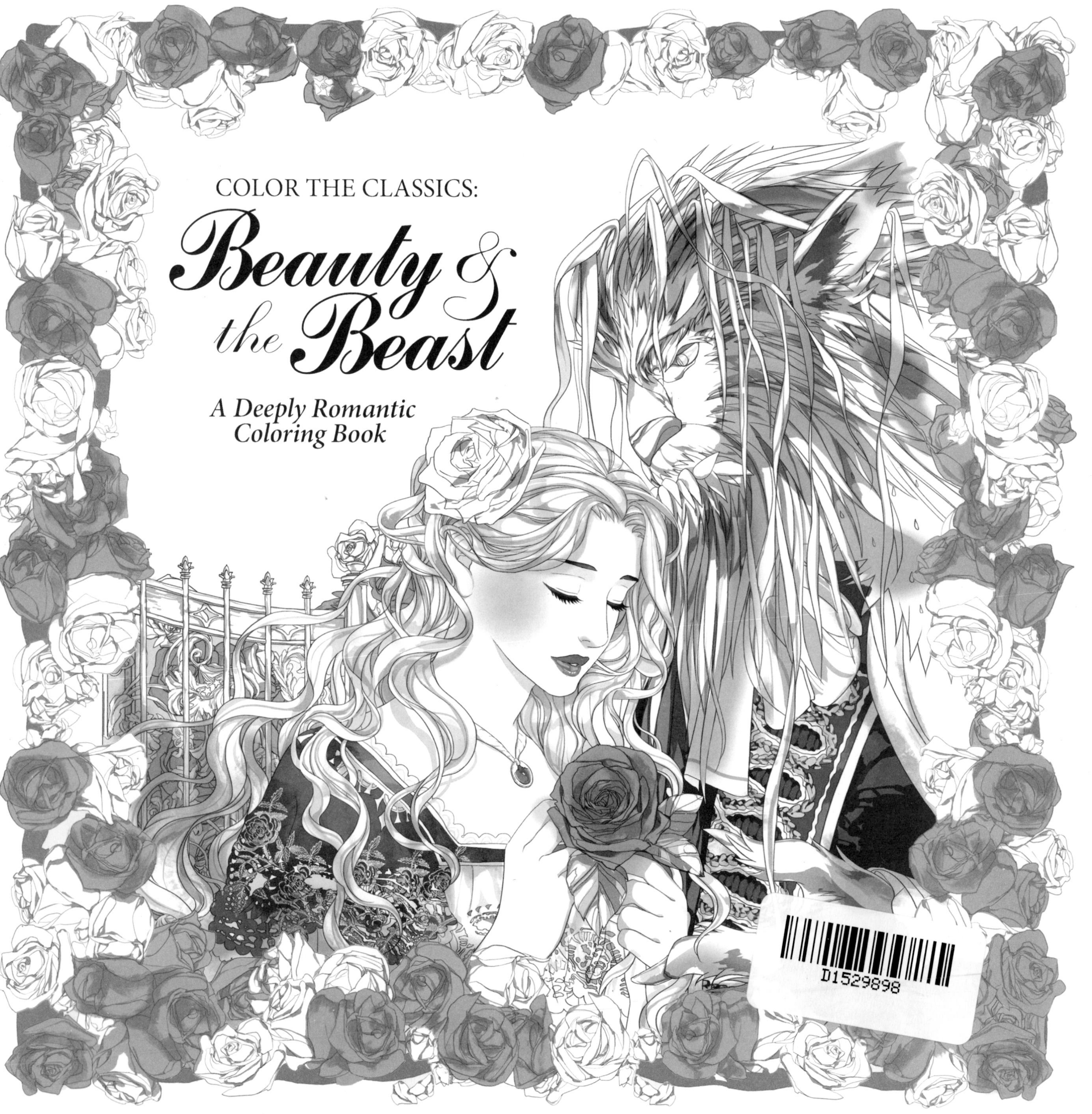

Translation: Lauren Na
Adaptation: Shanti Whitesides
Artwork Touch-Up: Meaghan Tucker
Cover Design: Nicky Lim
Production Manager: Lissa Pattillo
Editor-in-Chief: Adam Arnold
Publisher: Jason DeAngelis

Waves of Color books may be purchased in bulk for educational,
business, or promotional use. For information on bulk purchases,
please contact Macmillan Corporate & Premium Sales Department at
1-800-221-7945 (ext 5442) or write specialmarkets@macmillan.com.

ISBN: 978-1-626923-93-5

Printed in Canada

First Printing: May 2016

10 9 8 7 6 5 4 3 2 1

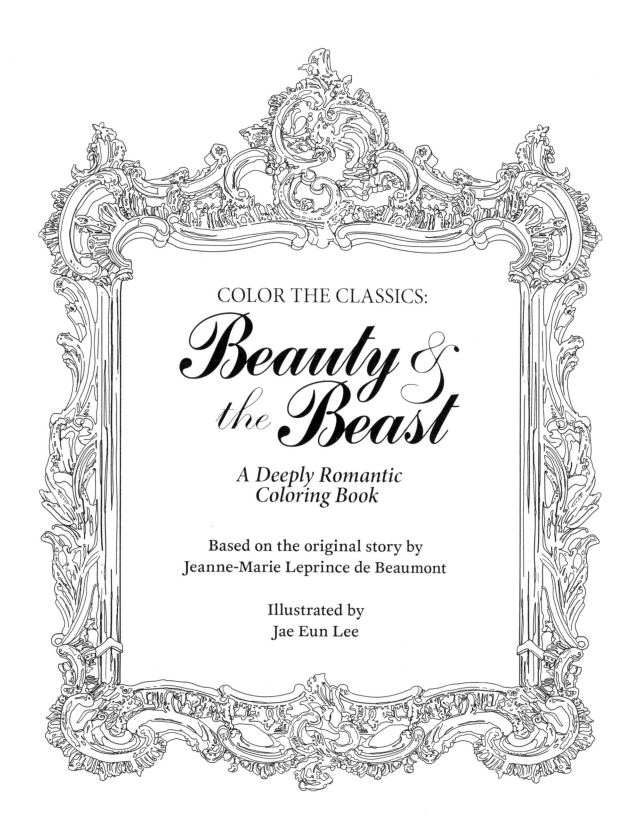

COLOR THE CLASSICS:

Beauty & the Beast

A Deeply Romantic Coloring Book

Based on the original story by
Jeanne-Marie Leprince de Beaumont

Illustrated by
Jae Eun Lee

Waves of Color

FOREWORD

Beauty and the Beast is a beautiful love story that has fascinated readers all over the world for centuries. What few people know is that this enduring fairy tale is actually loosely based on the Greek tale of Cupid and Psyche. Gabrielle-Suzanne Barbot de Villeneuve took inspiration from that myth to write the first version of *Beauty and the Beast* in 1740. Later, in 1756, the French novelist Jeanne-Marie Leprince de Beaumont abridged and rewrote Barbot de Villeneuve's lengthy work, popularizing the story for the world at large.

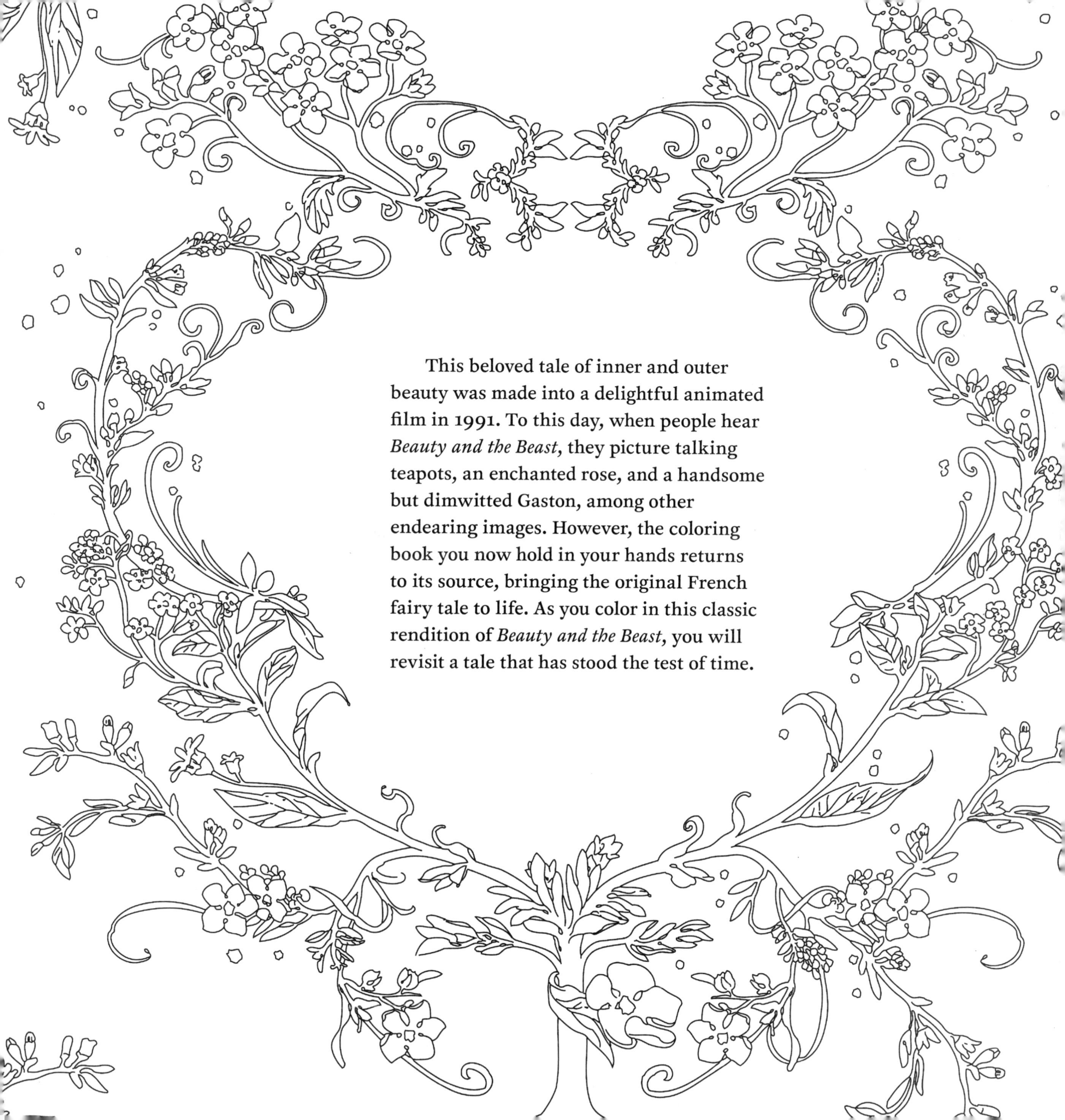

This beloved tale of inner and outer beauty was made into a delightful animated film in 1991. To this day, when people hear *Beauty and the Beast,* they picture talking teapots, an enchanted rose, and a handsome but dimwitted Gaston, among other endearing images. However, the coloring book you now hold in your hands returns to its source, bringing the original French fairy tale to life. As you color in this classic rendition of *Beauty and the Beast,* you will revisit a tale that has stood the test of time.

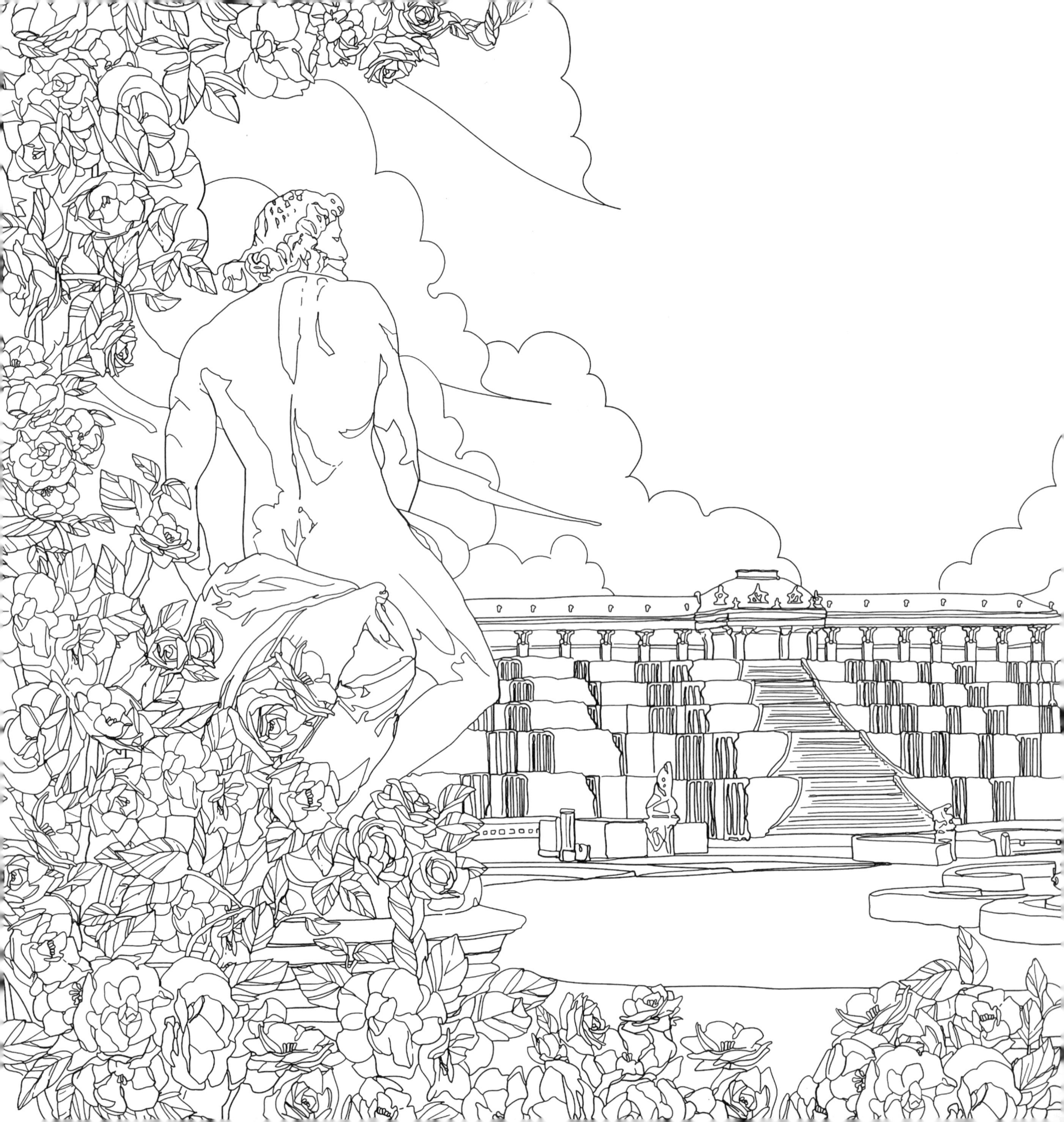

There was once a merchant, who was very, very rich. He had six children, three boys and three girls. His daughters were all beautiful, but his youngest one was especially admired, and from the time she was a small child, had been only known and spoken of as "Beauty."

The young girl was not only more beautiful than her sisters, but also kinder and more amiable.

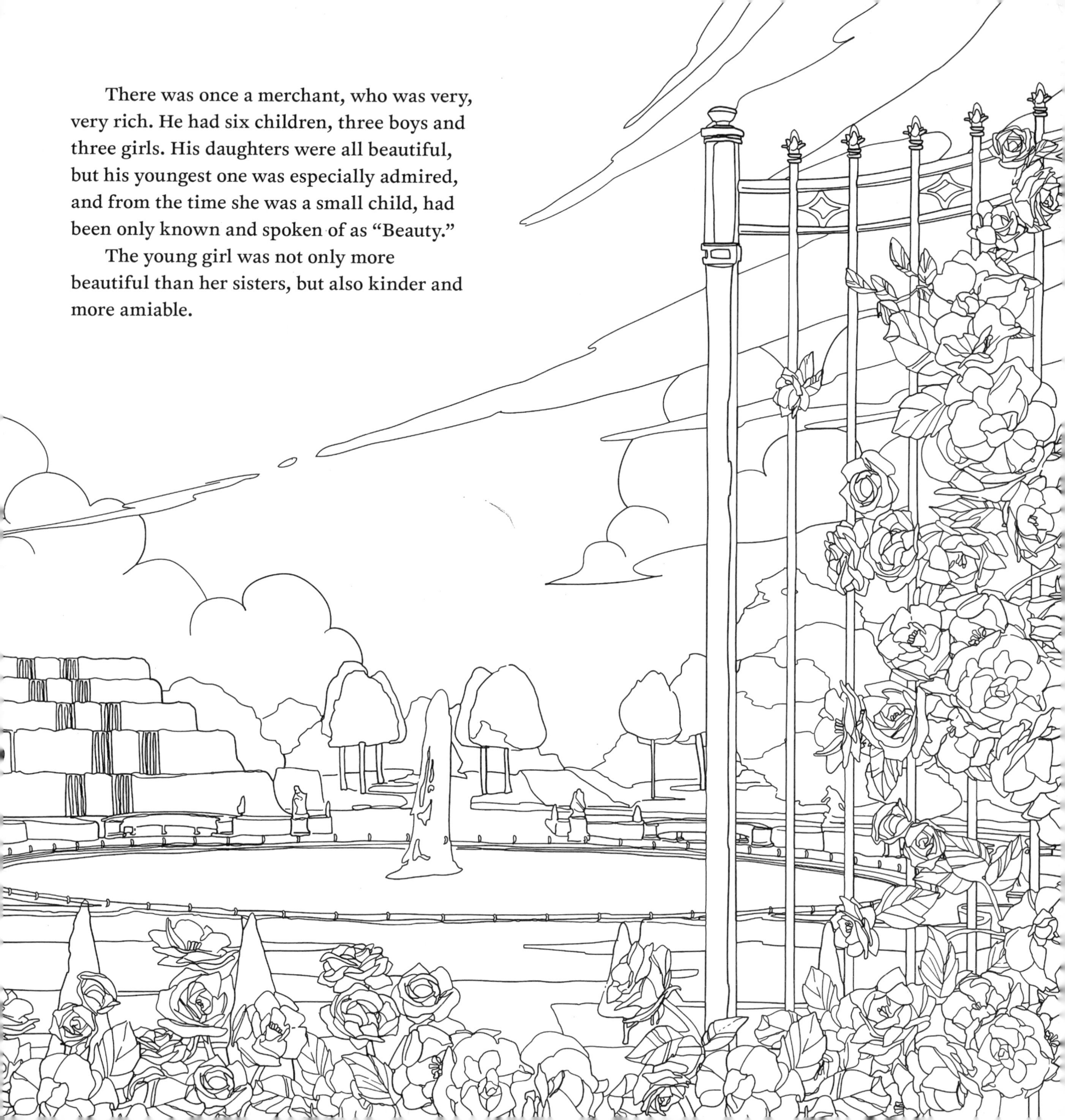

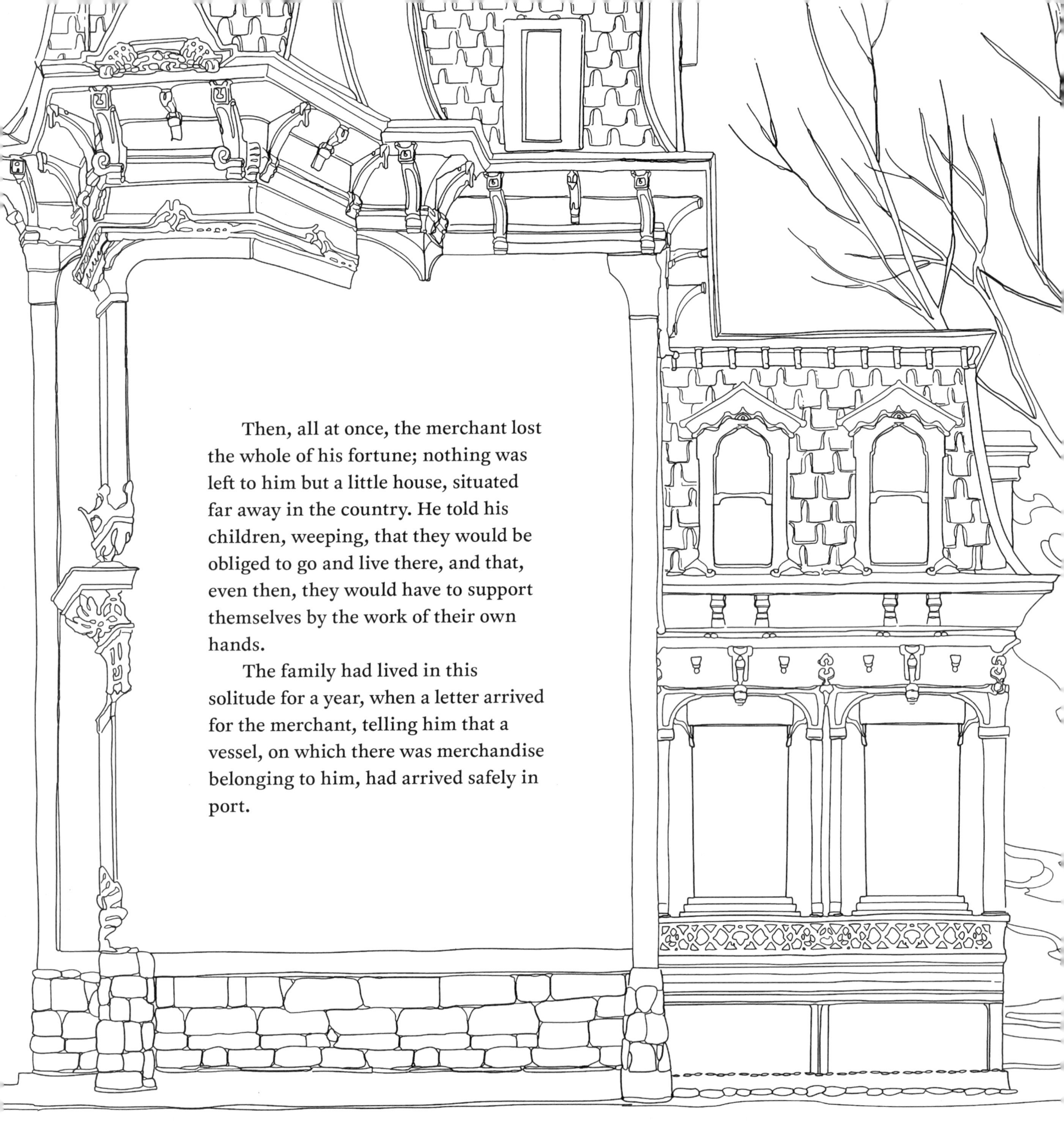

Then, all at once, the merchant lost the whole of his fortune; nothing was left to him but a little house, situated far away in the country. He told his children, weeping, that they would be obliged to go and live there, and that, even then, they would have to support themselves by the work of their own hands.

The family had lived in this solitude for a year, when a letter arrived for the merchant, telling him that a vessel, on which there was merchandise belonging to him, had arrived safely in port.

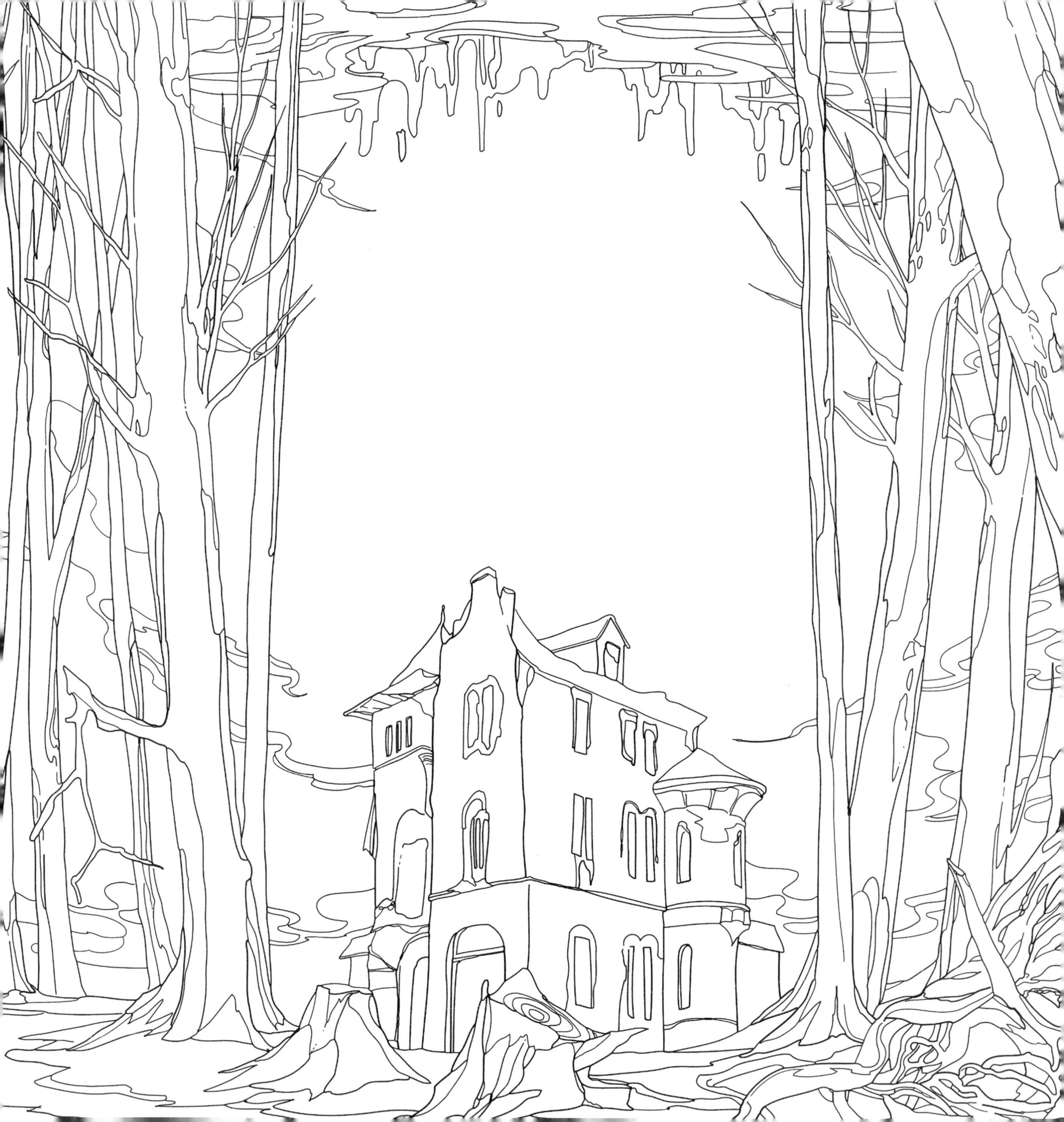

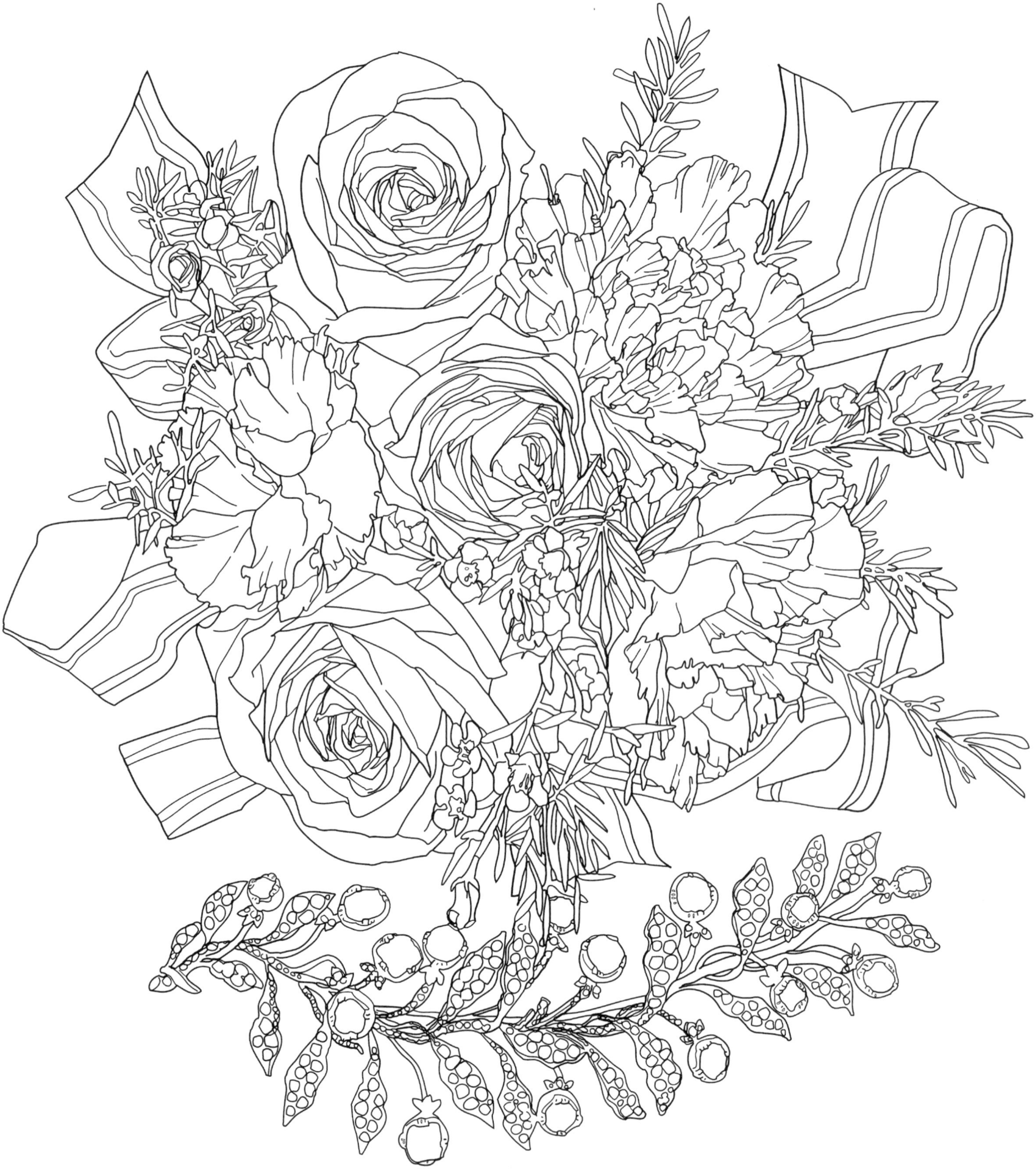

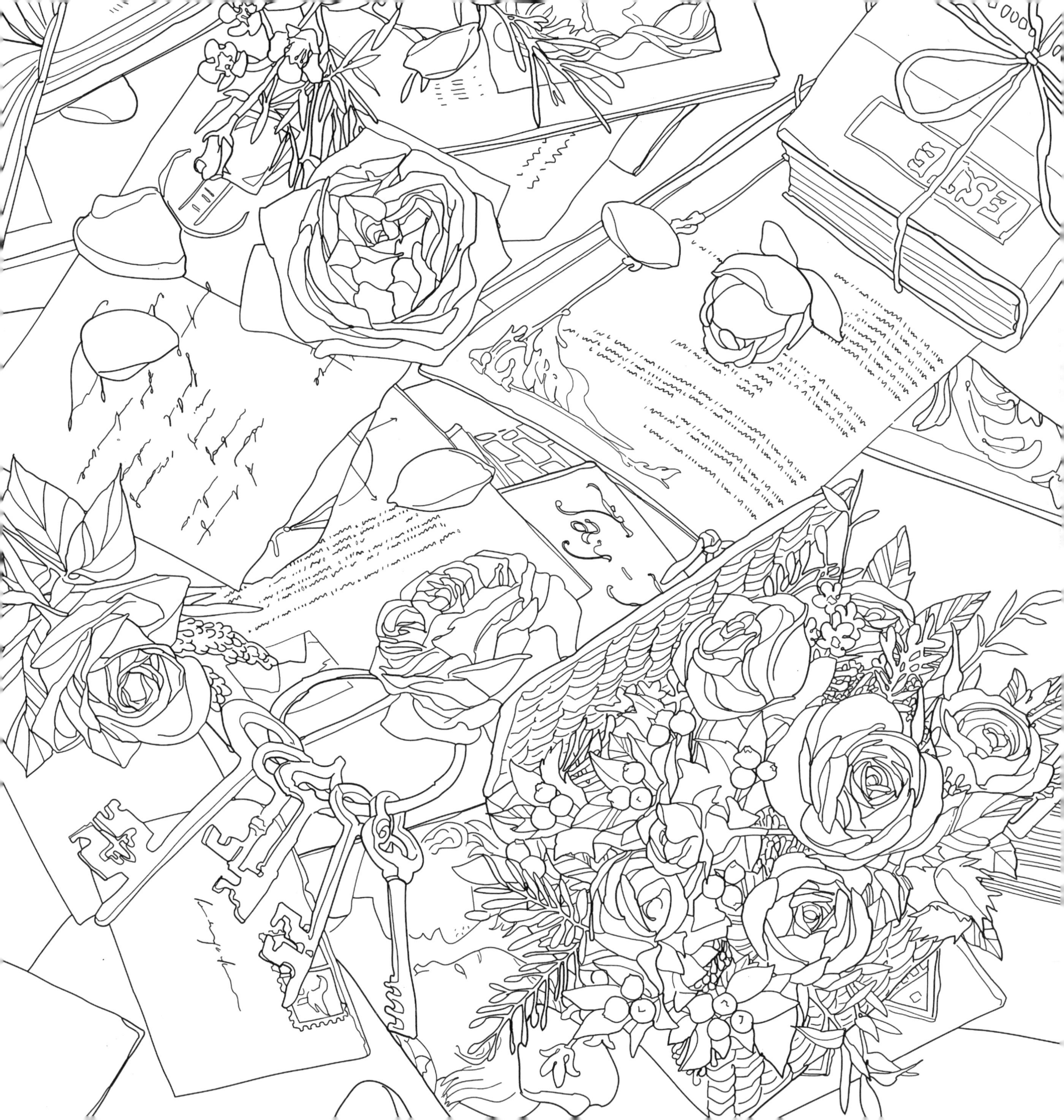

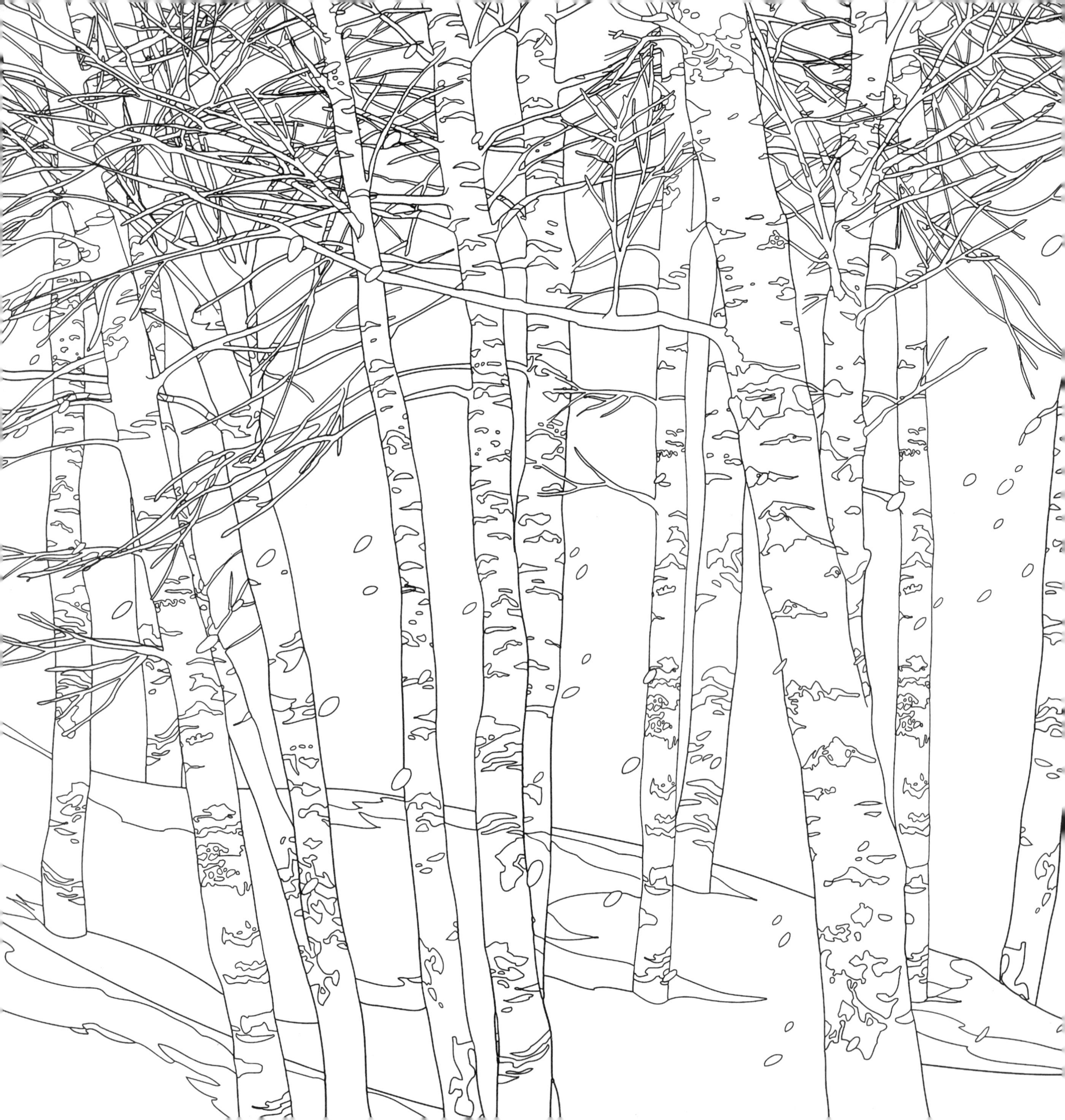

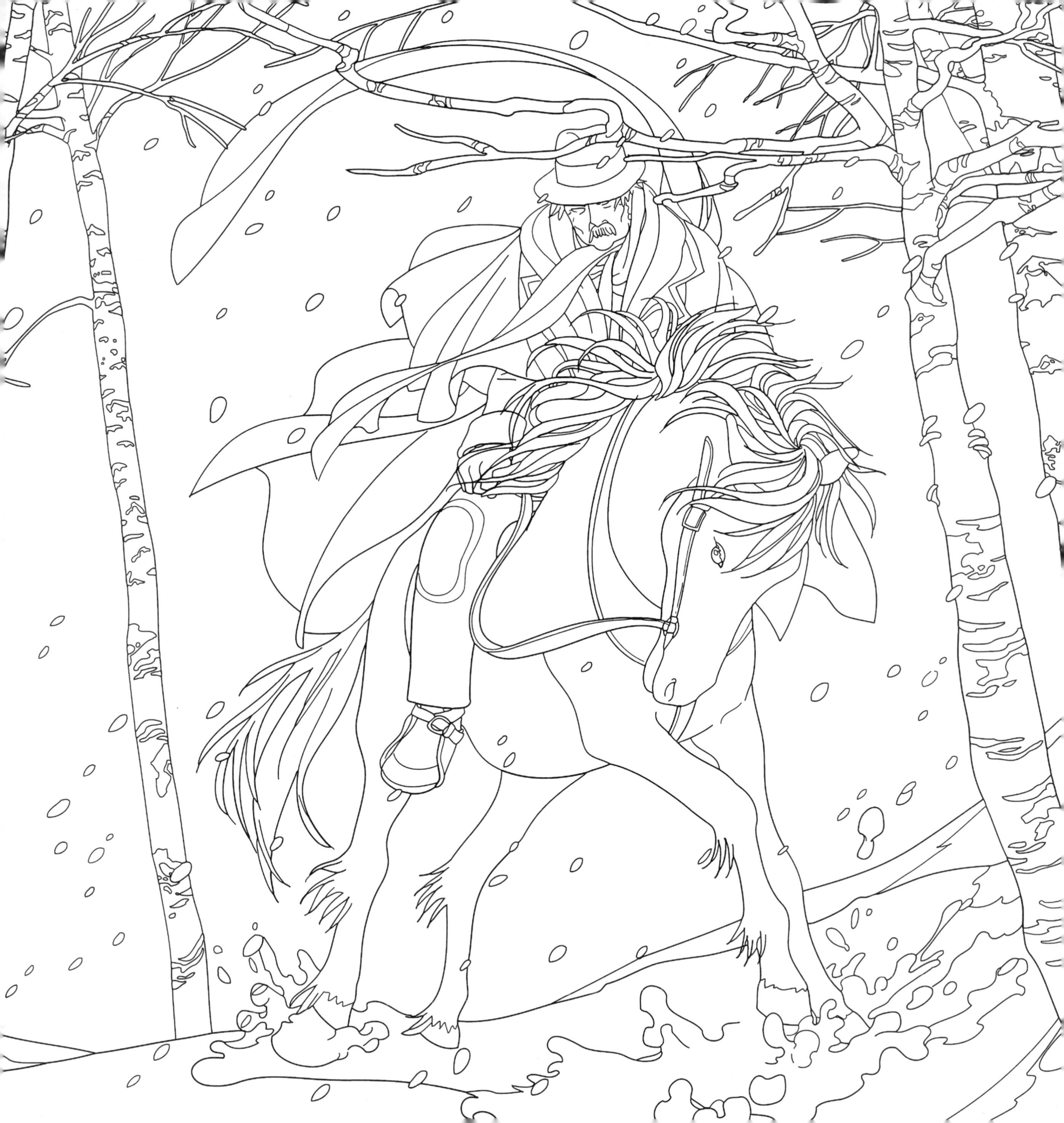

The father left them, but on arriving at his destination, he had to go to law about his merchandise, and after a great deal of trouble, he turned back home as poor as he came. He had not many more miles to go, and was already enjoying, in anticipation, the pleasure of seeing his children again, when, passing on his journey through a large wood, he lost his way.

All at once, however, he caught sight of a bright light, which appeared to be some way off, at the further end of a long avenue of trees. He walked towards it, and soon saw that it came from a splendid castle, which was brilliantly illuminated.

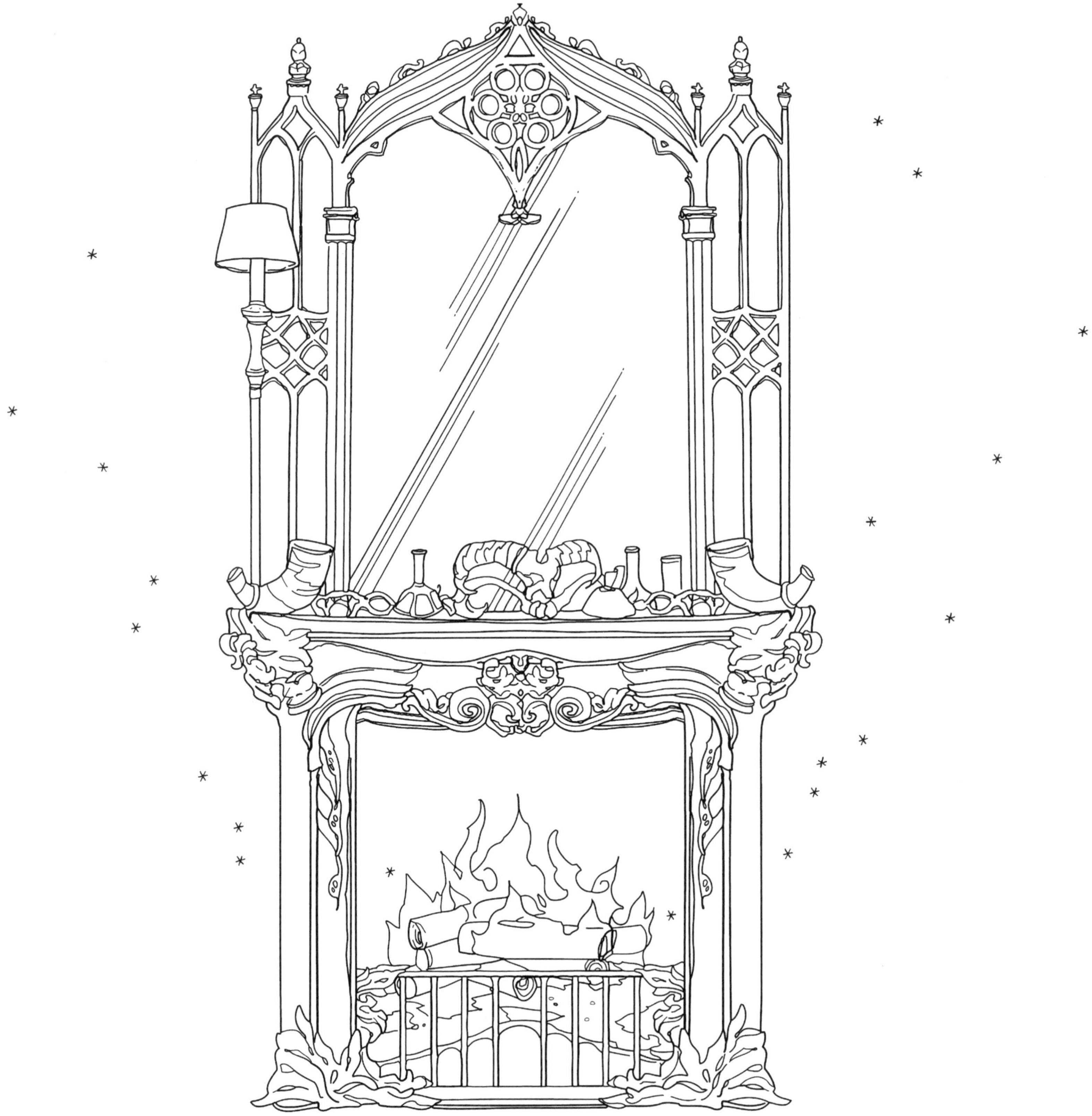

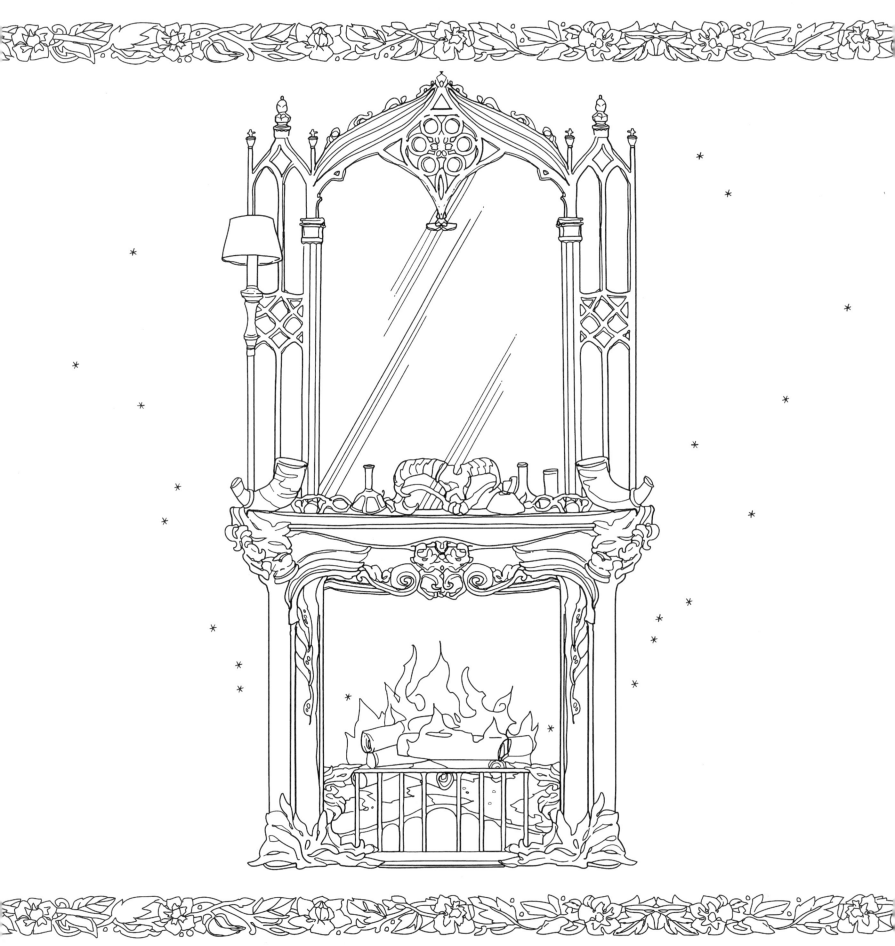

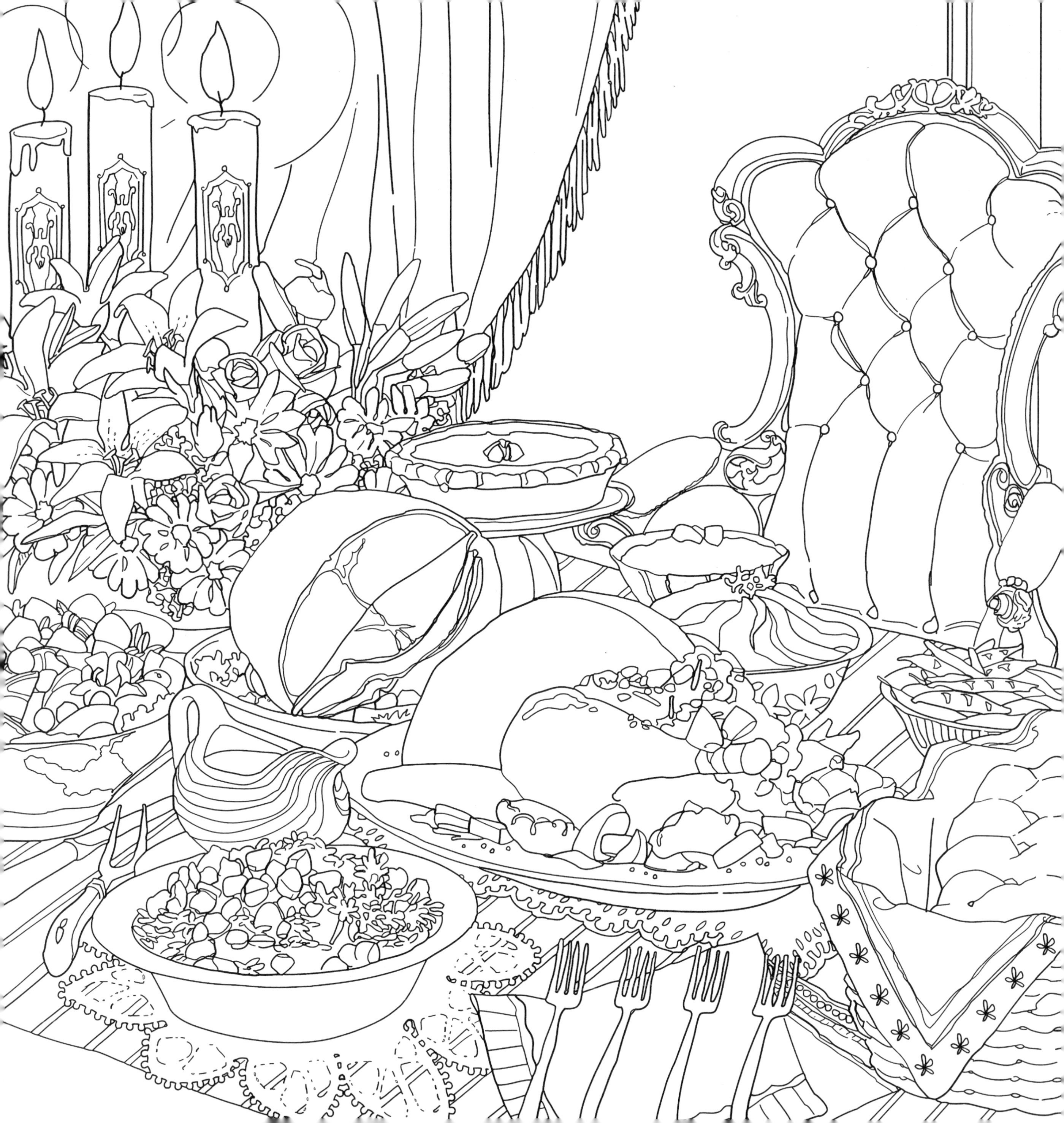

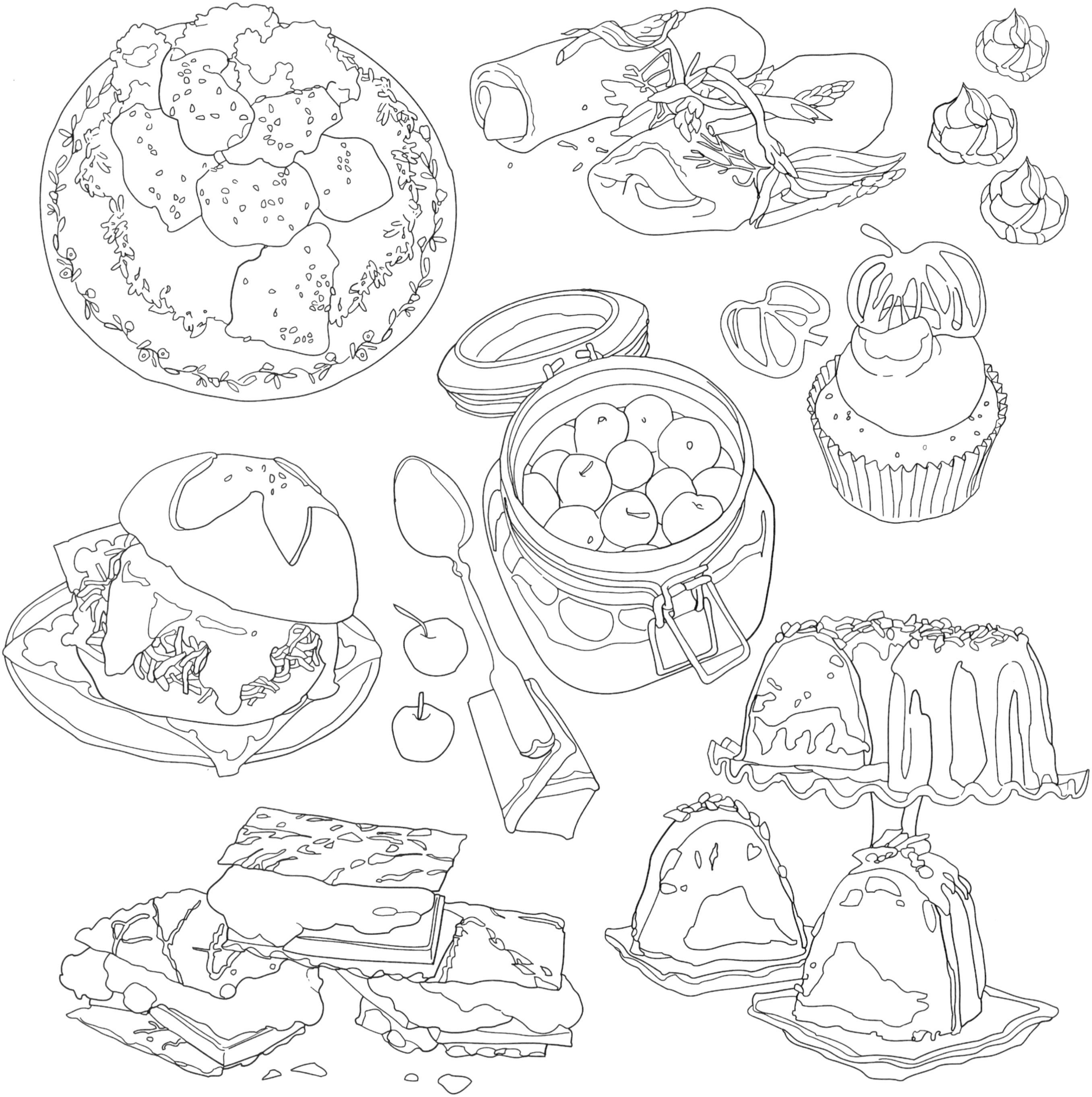

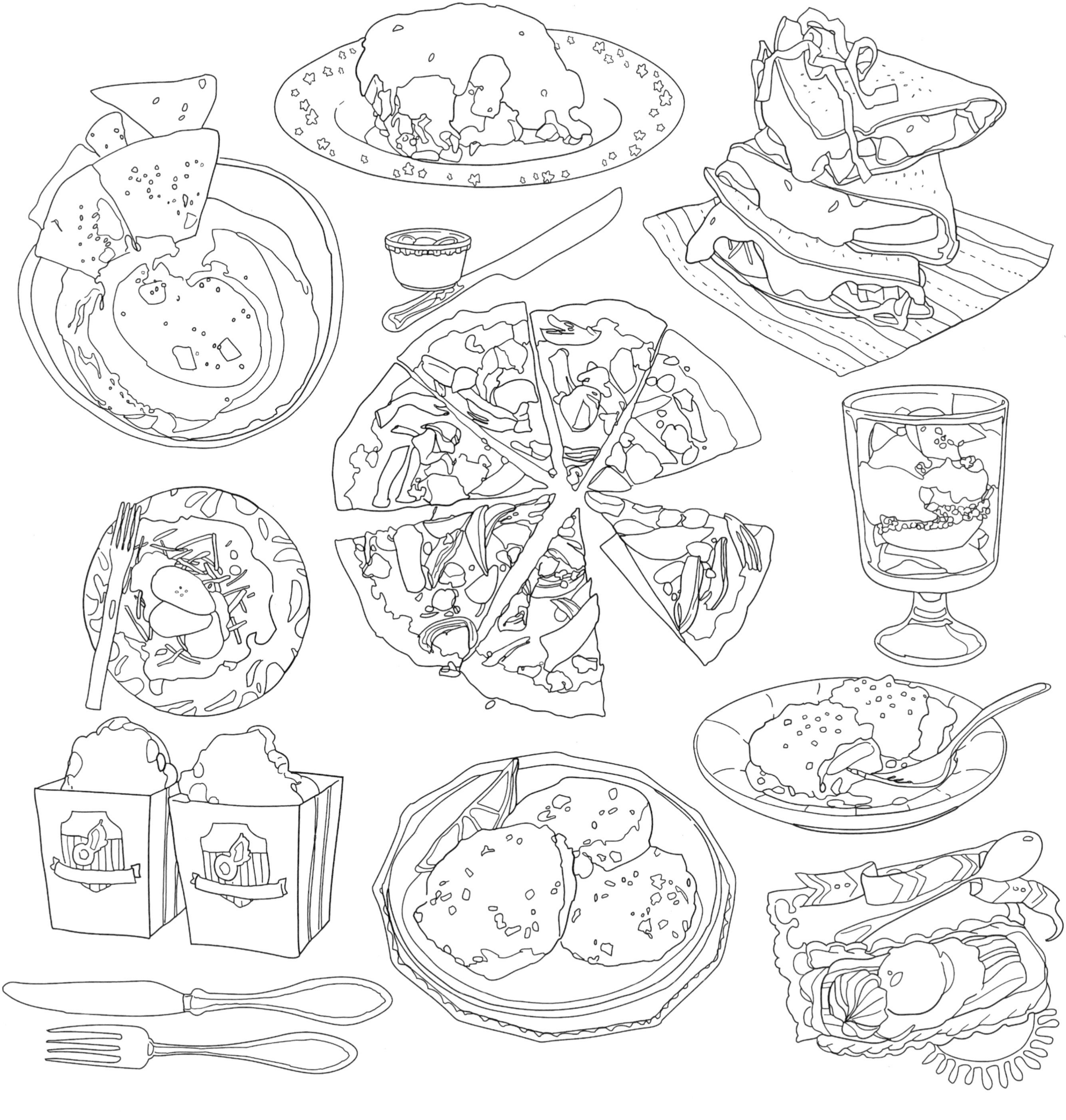

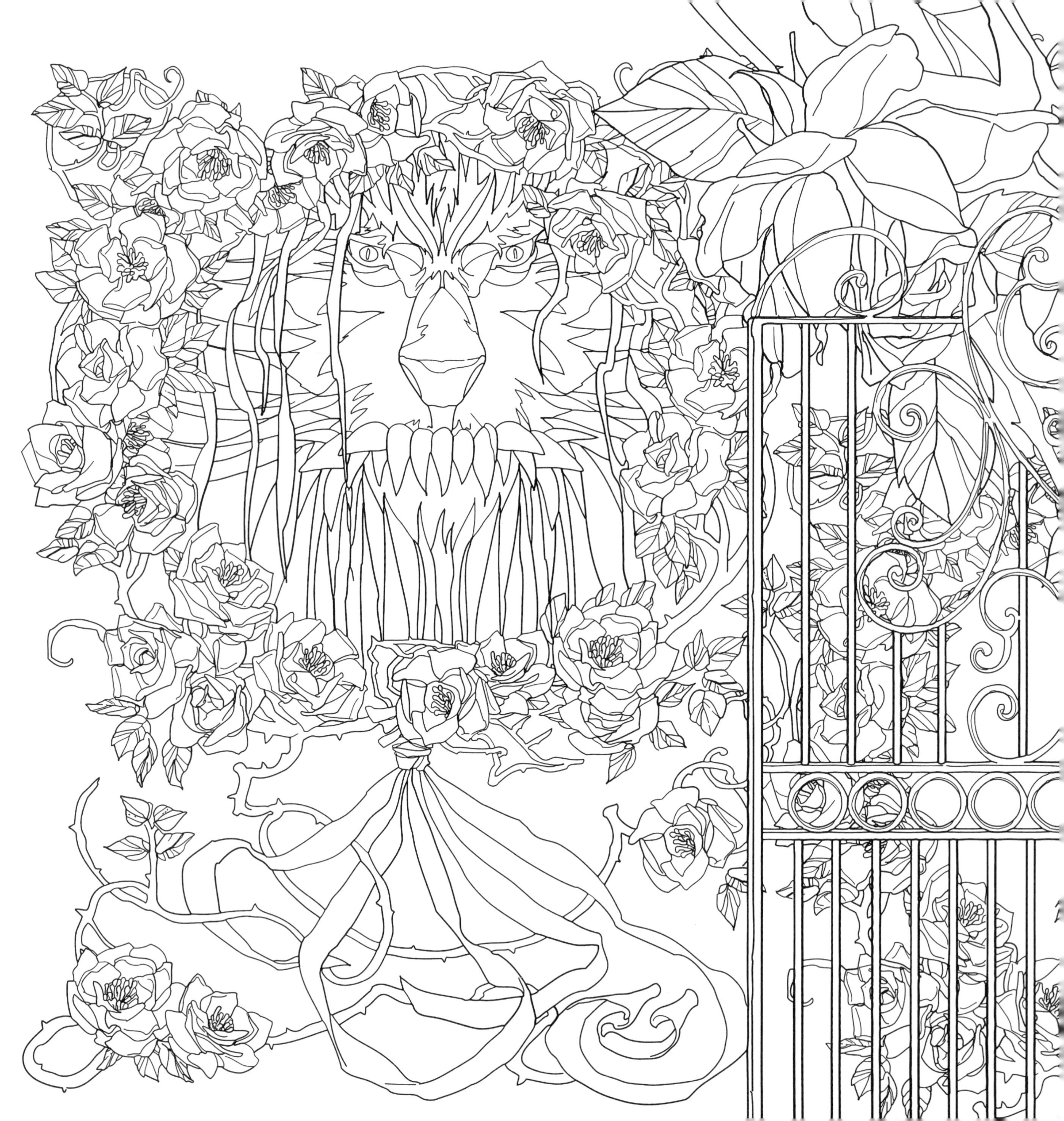

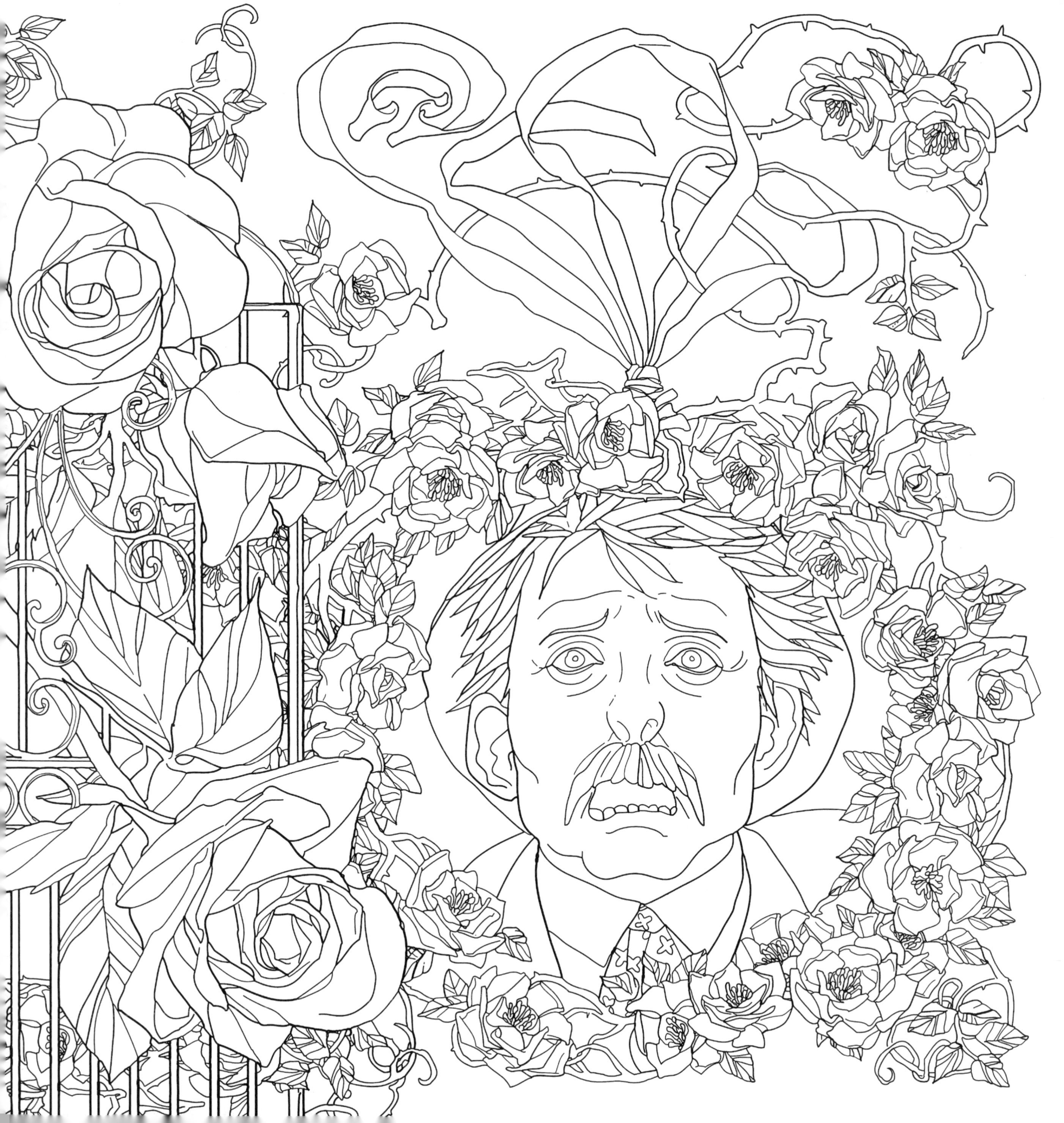

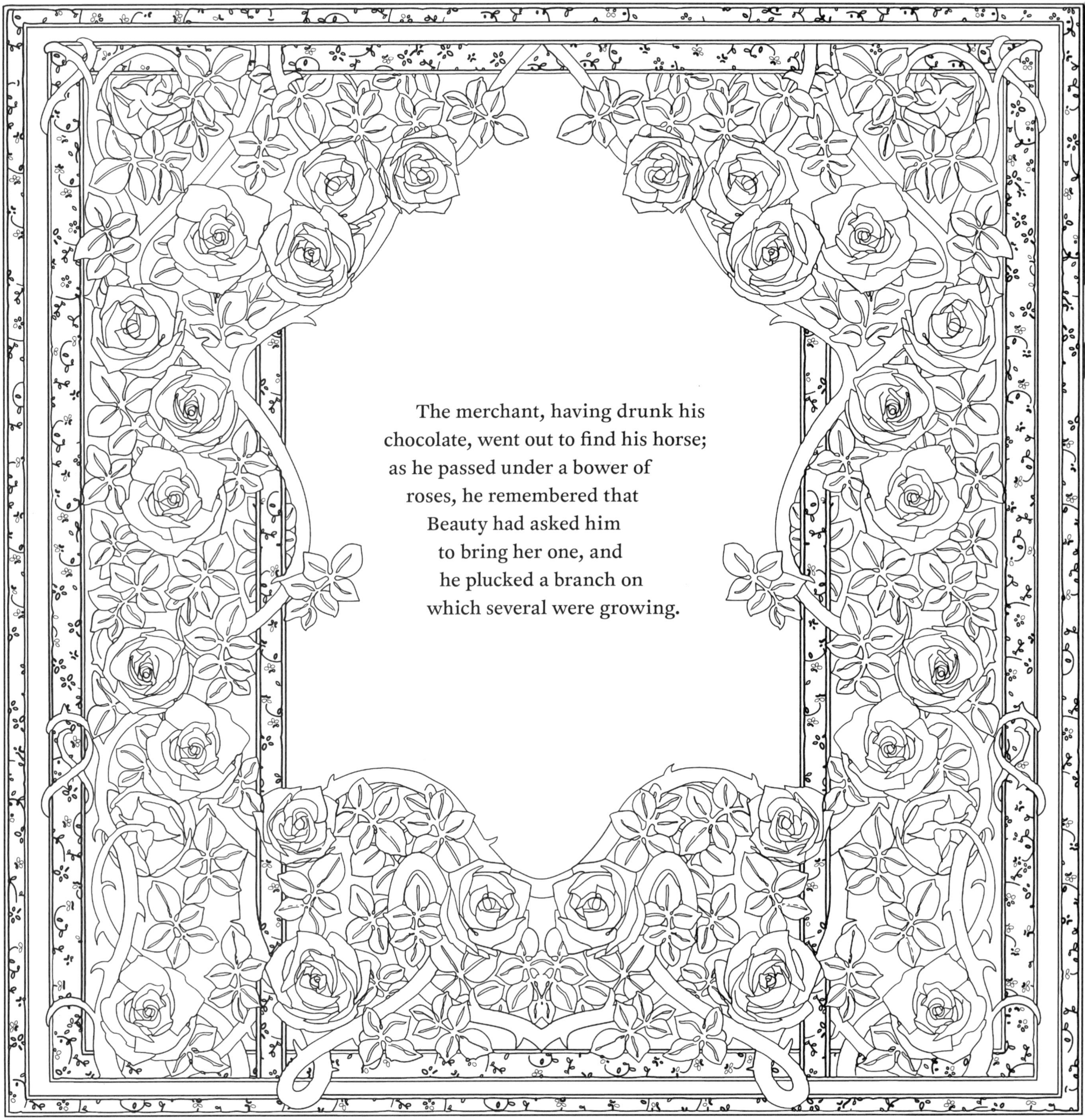

The merchant, having drunk his chocolate, went out to find his horse; as he passed under a bower of roses, he remembered that Beauty had asked him to bring her one, and he plucked a branch on which several were growing.

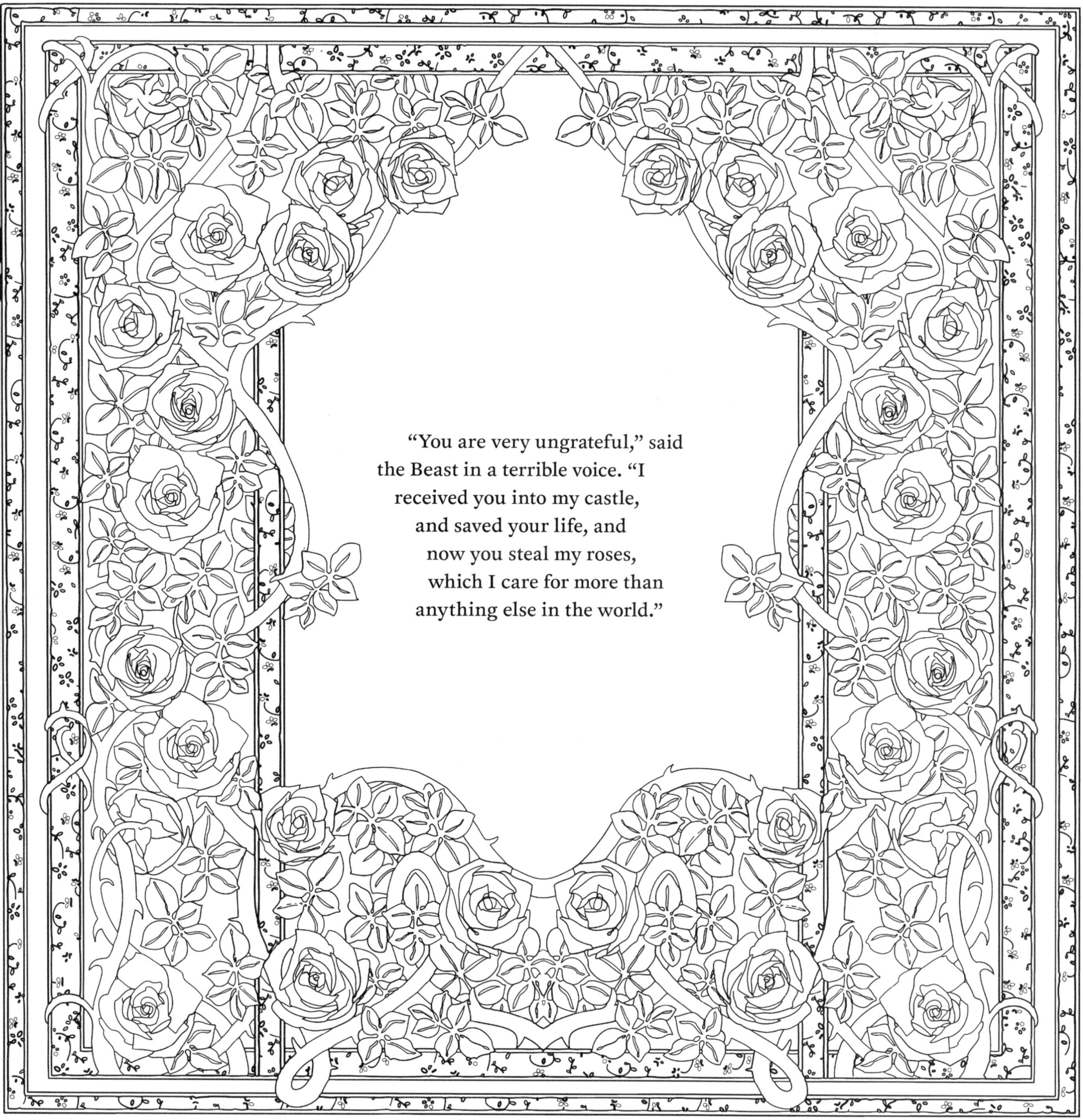

“You are very ungrateful,” said the Beast in a terrible voice. “I received you into my castle, and saved your life, and now you steal my roses, which I care for more than anything else in the world.”

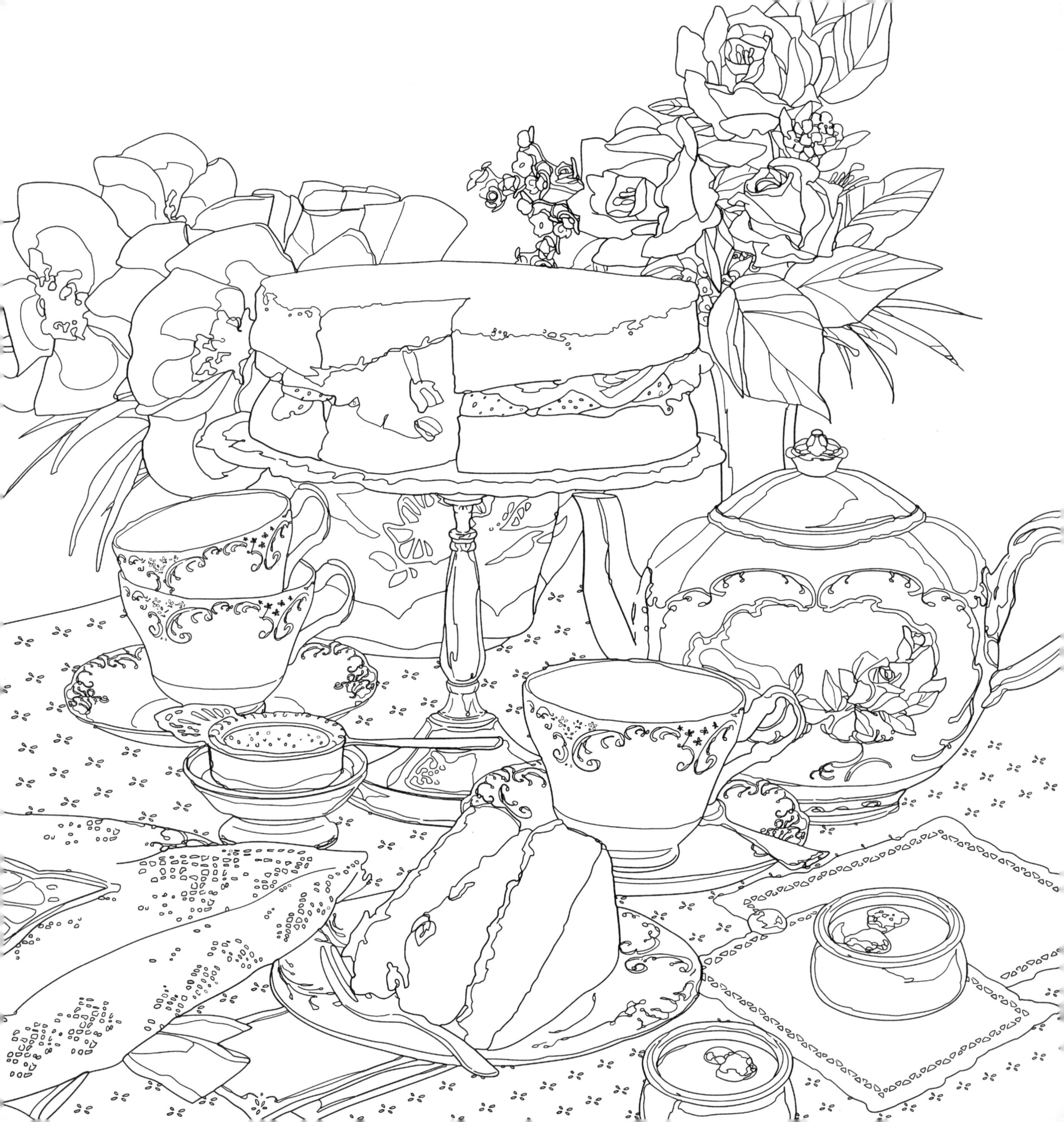

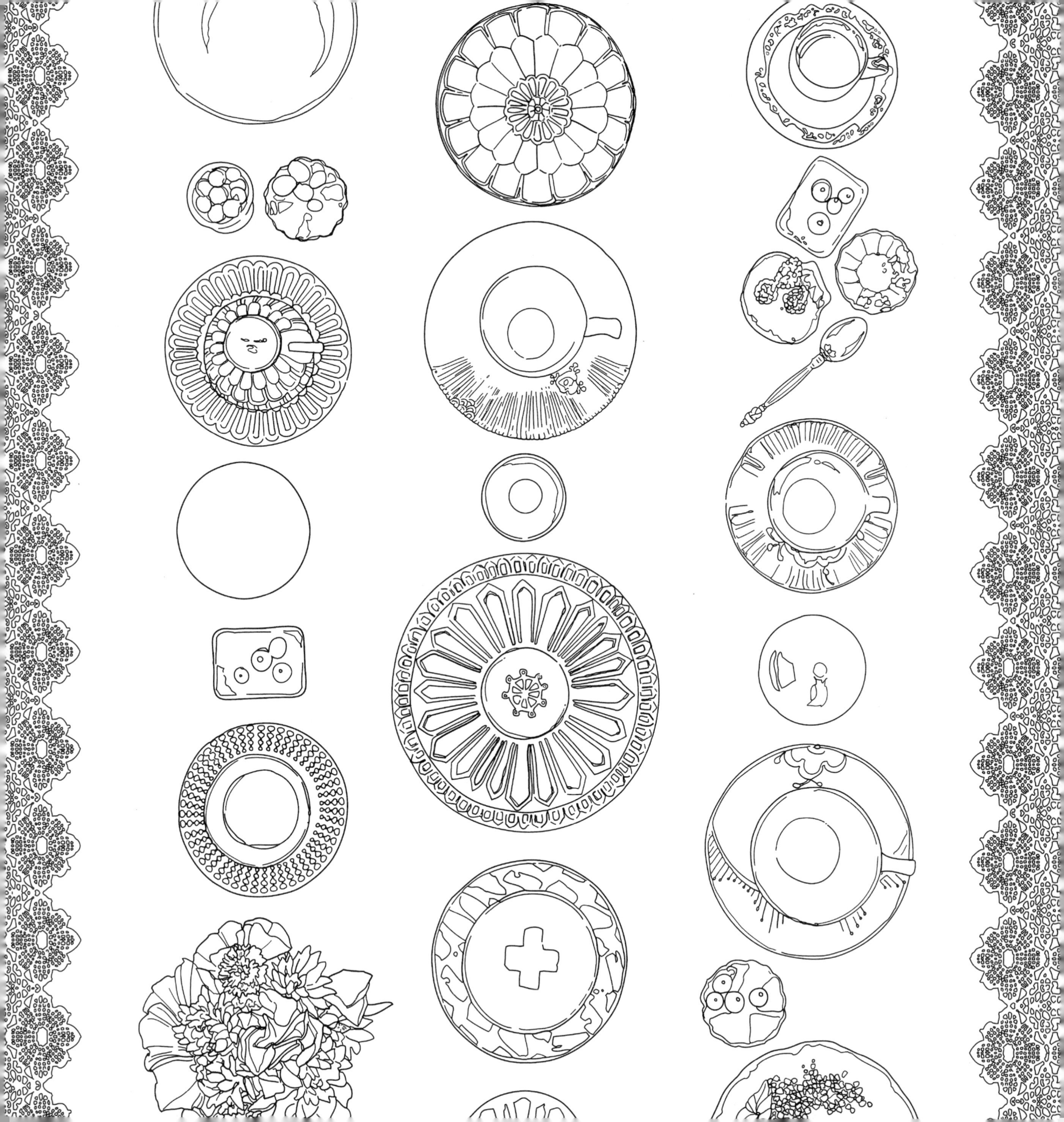

"But you tell me you have
some daughters; I will pardon you on
condition that one of your daughters
will come of her own free will to die in
your place. Do not stop to argue with me;
go! and if your daughter refuses to die
for you, swear that you will return
yourself in three months' time."

In vain the others tried to dissuade
her, Beauty persisted in her determination
to go to the castle; and her sisters were not
sorry about it.

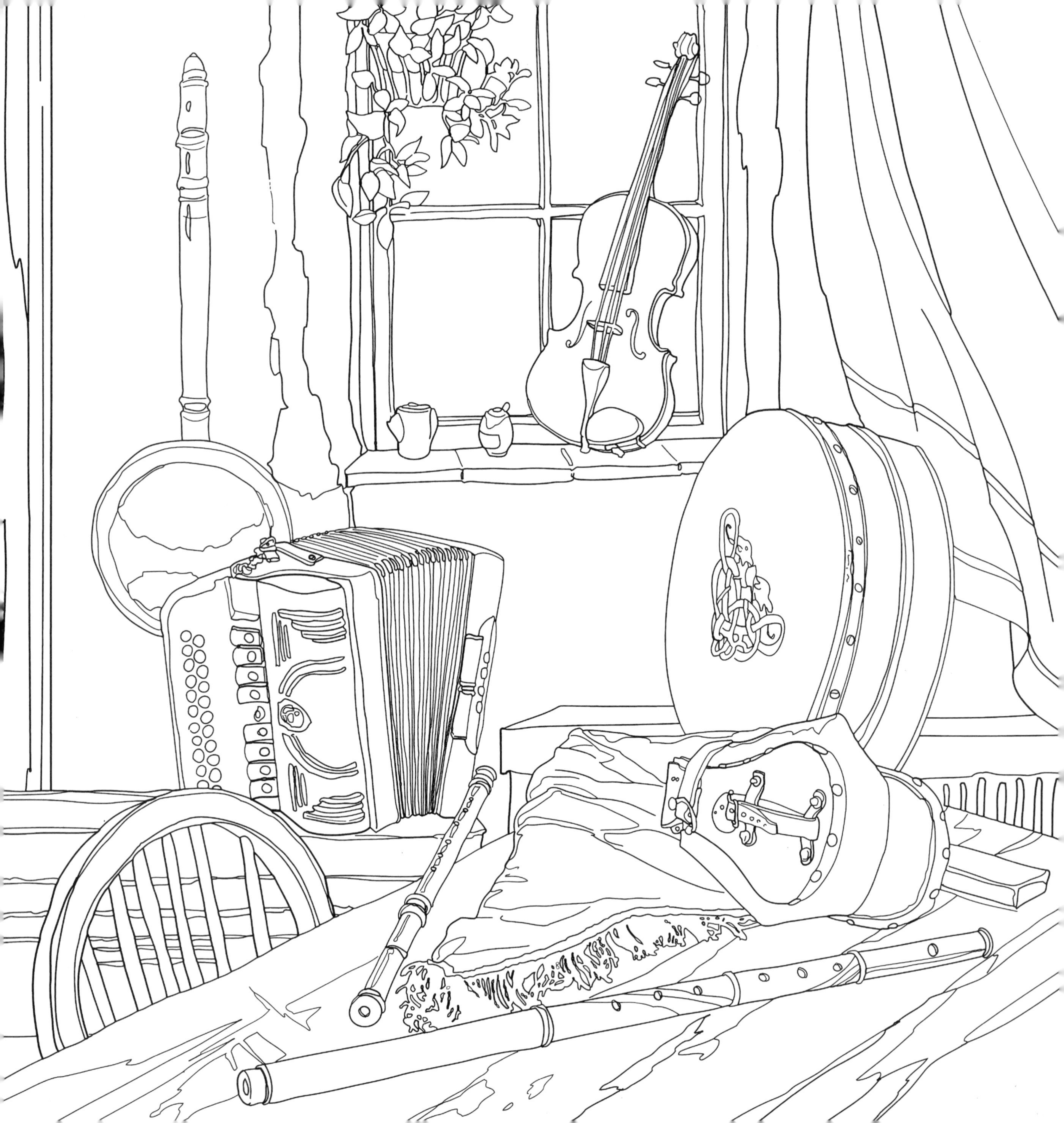

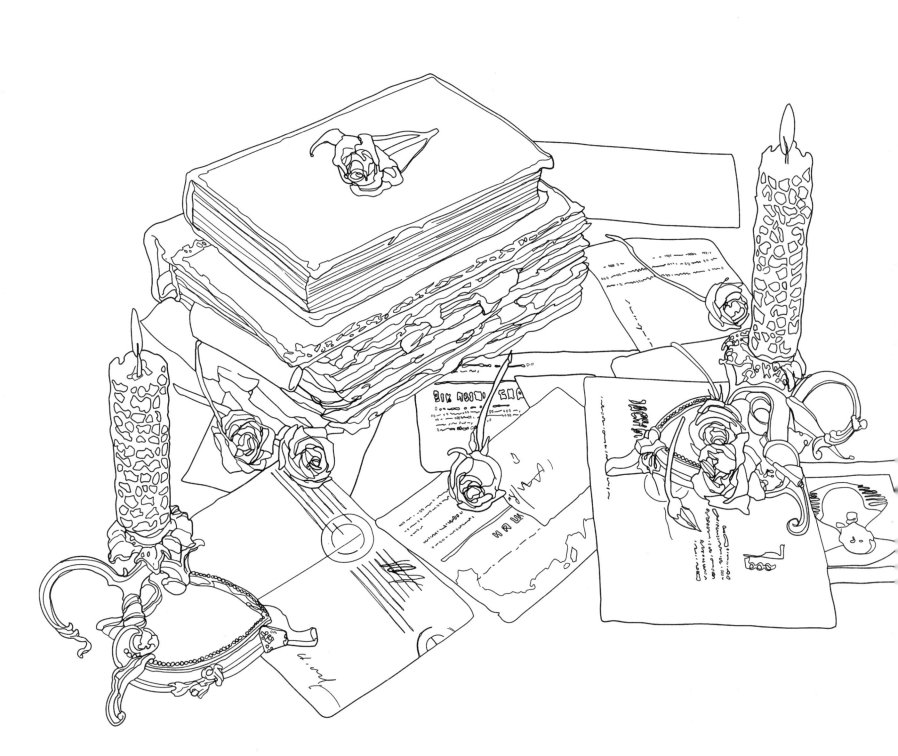

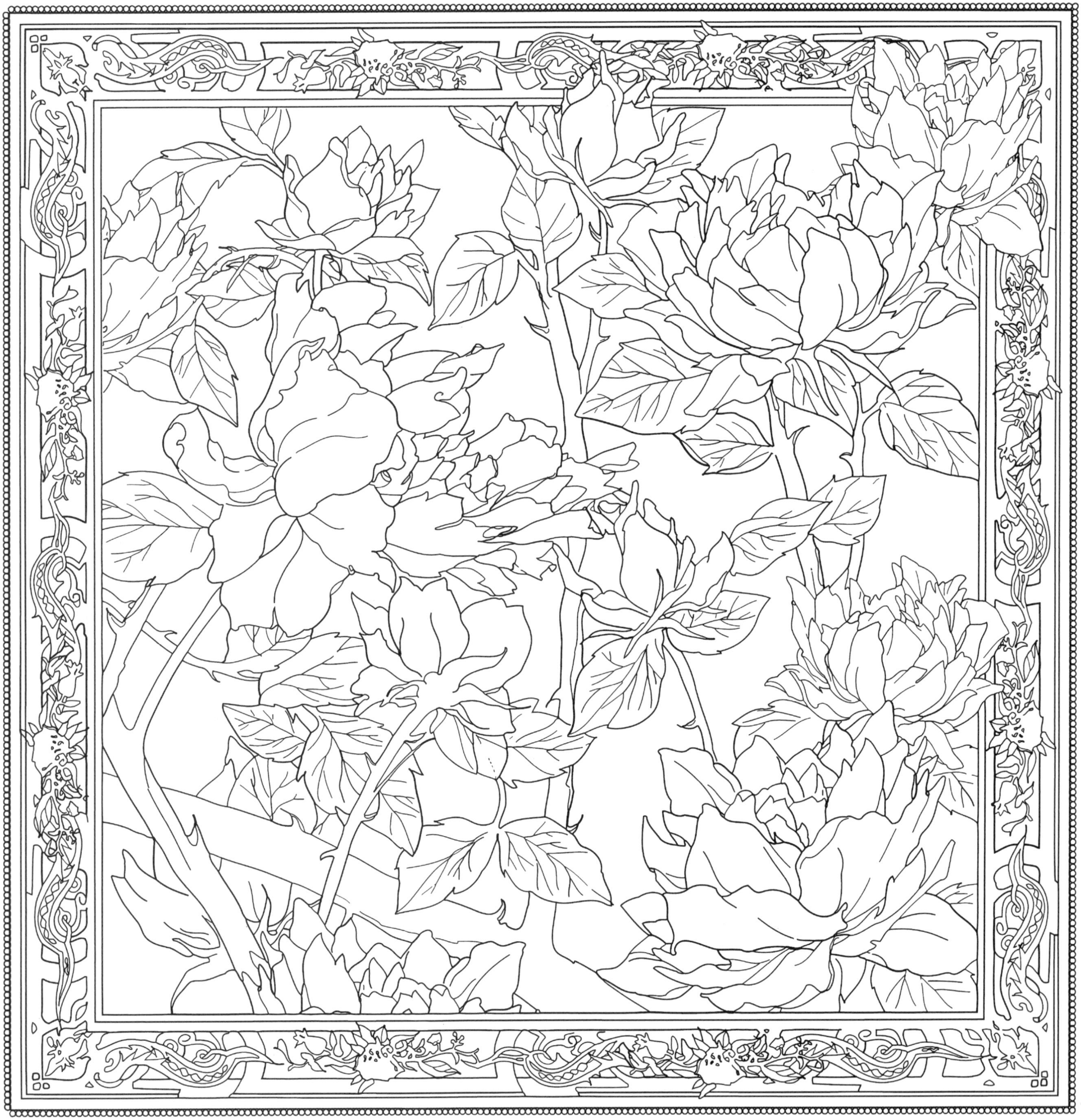

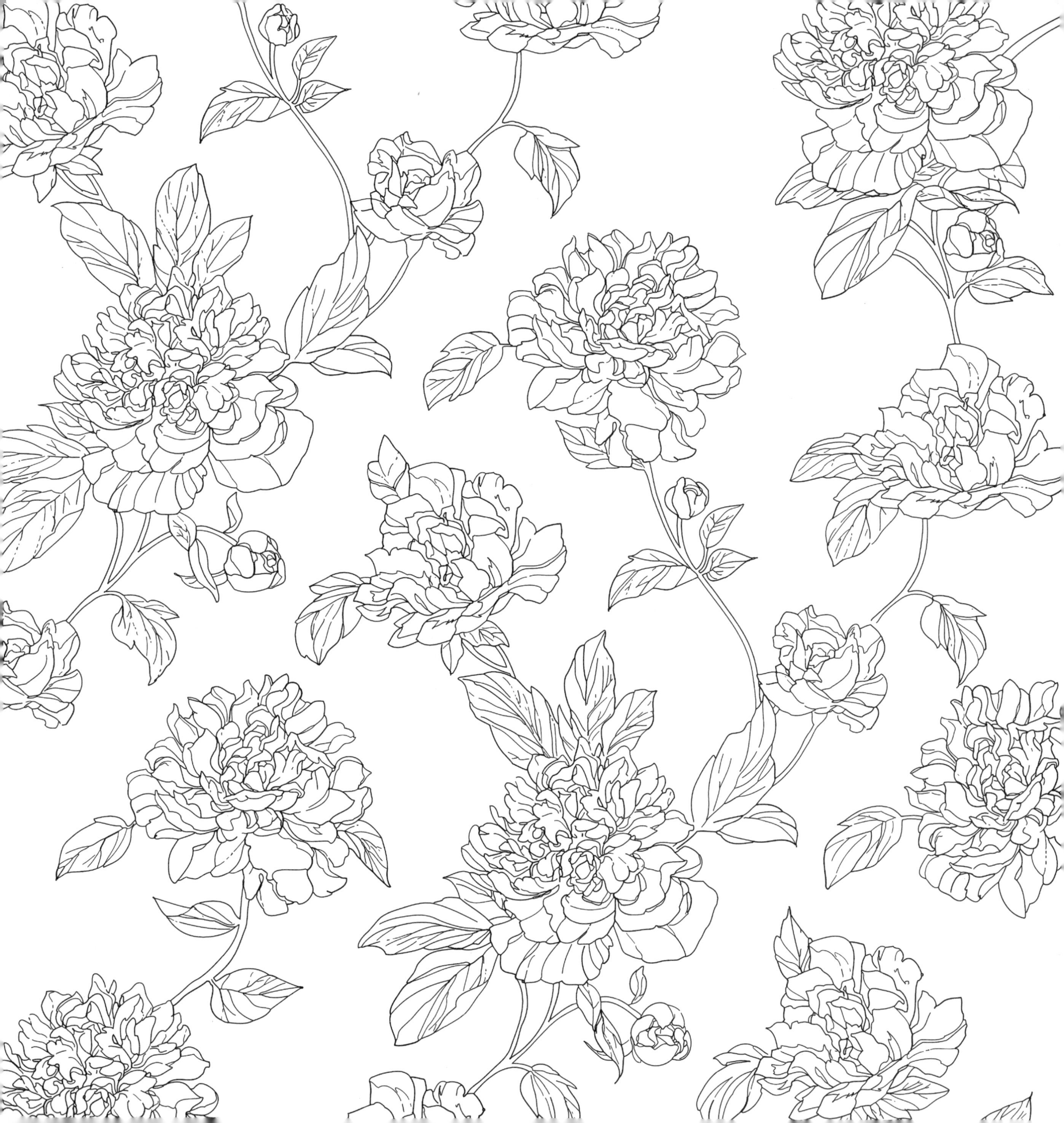

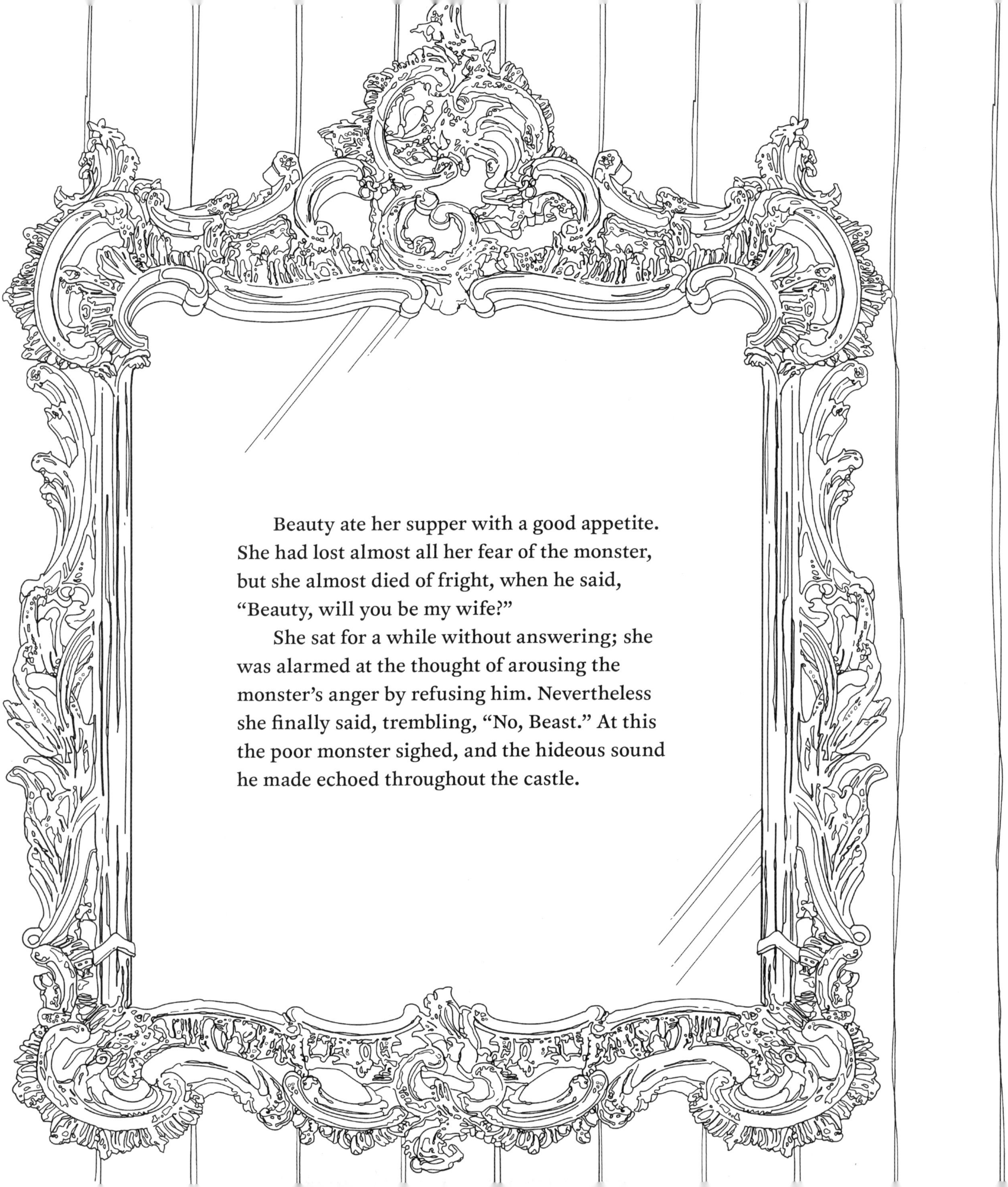

Beauty ate her supper with a good appetite. She had lost almost all her fear of the monster, but she almost died of fright, when he said, "Beauty, will you be my wife?"

She sat for a while without answering; she was alarmed at the thought of arousing the monster's anger by refusing him. Nevertheless she finally said, trembling, "No, Beast." At this the poor monster sighed, and the hideous sound he made echoed throughout the castle.

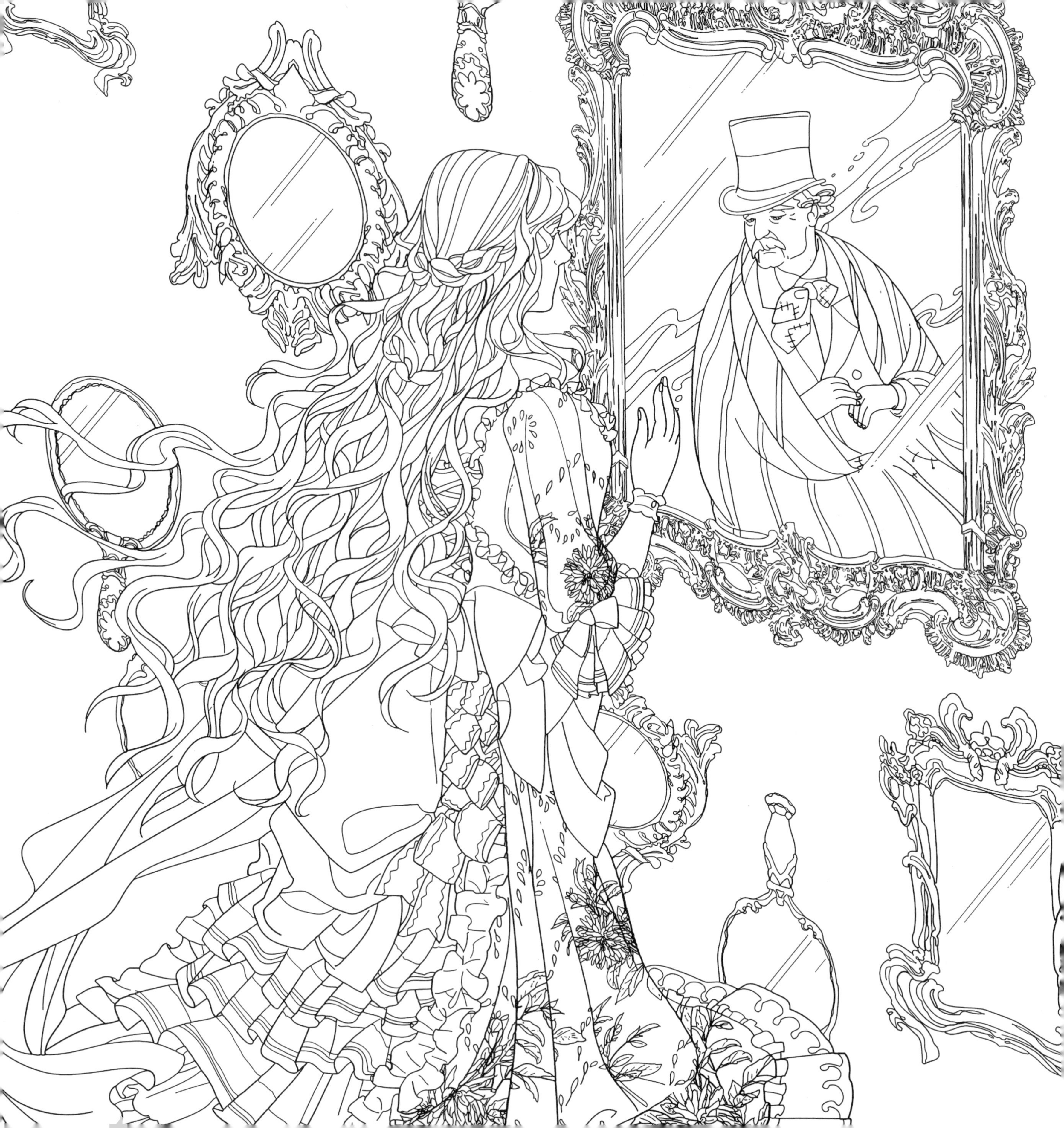

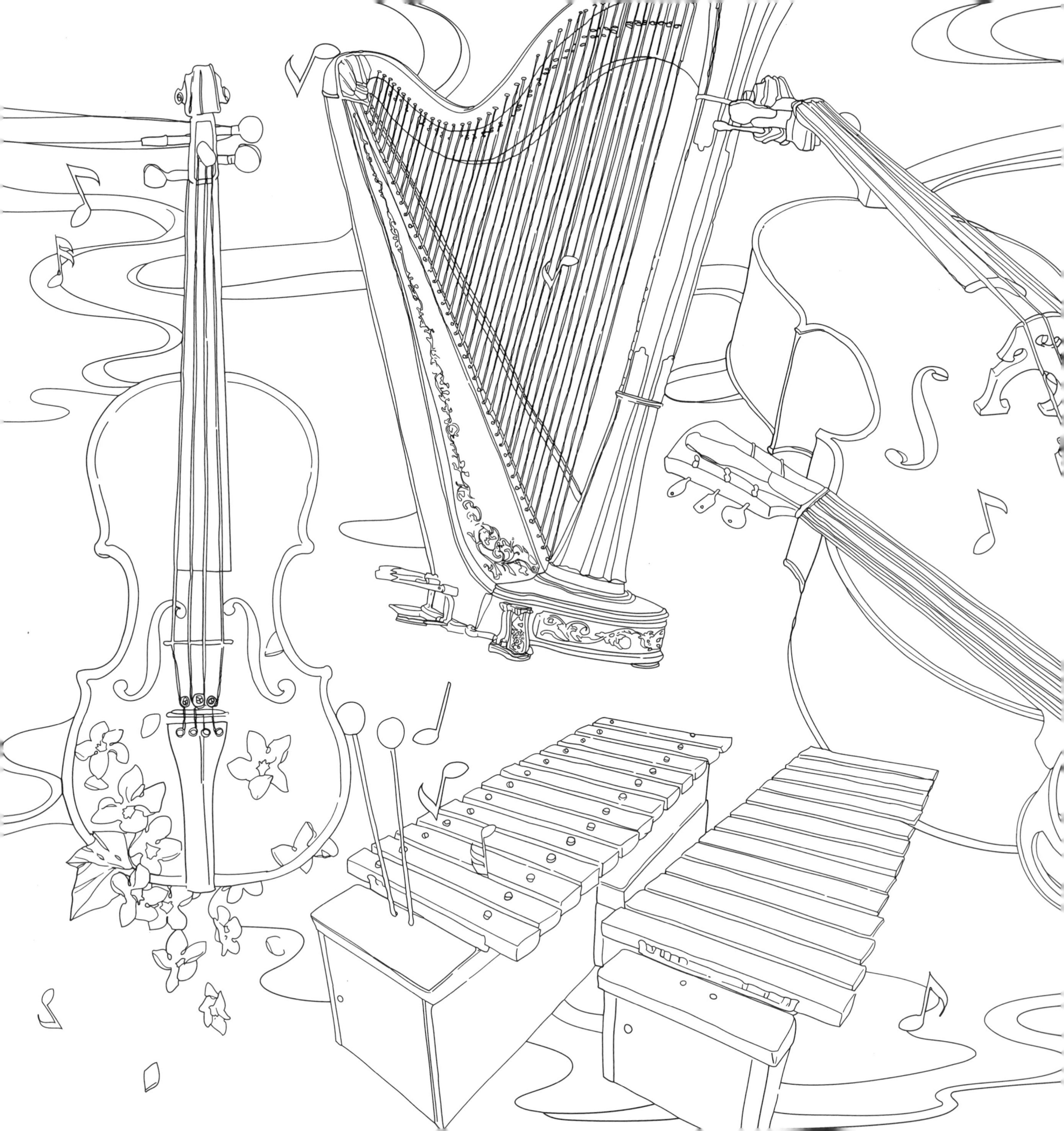

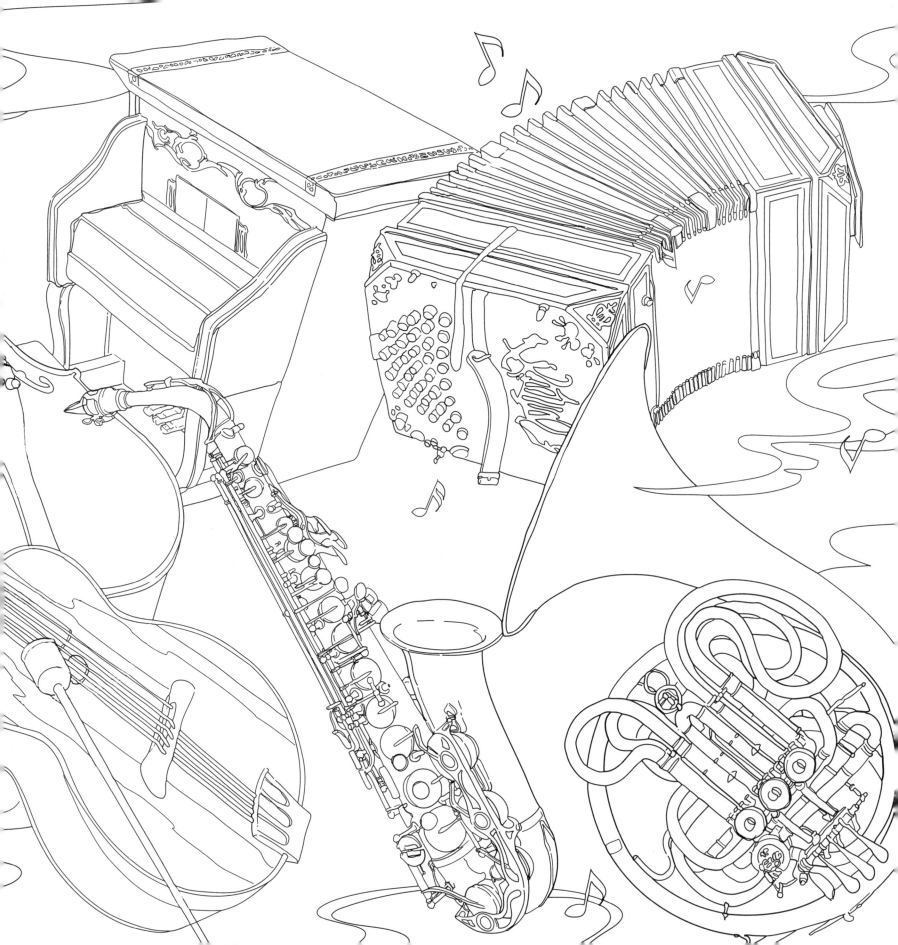

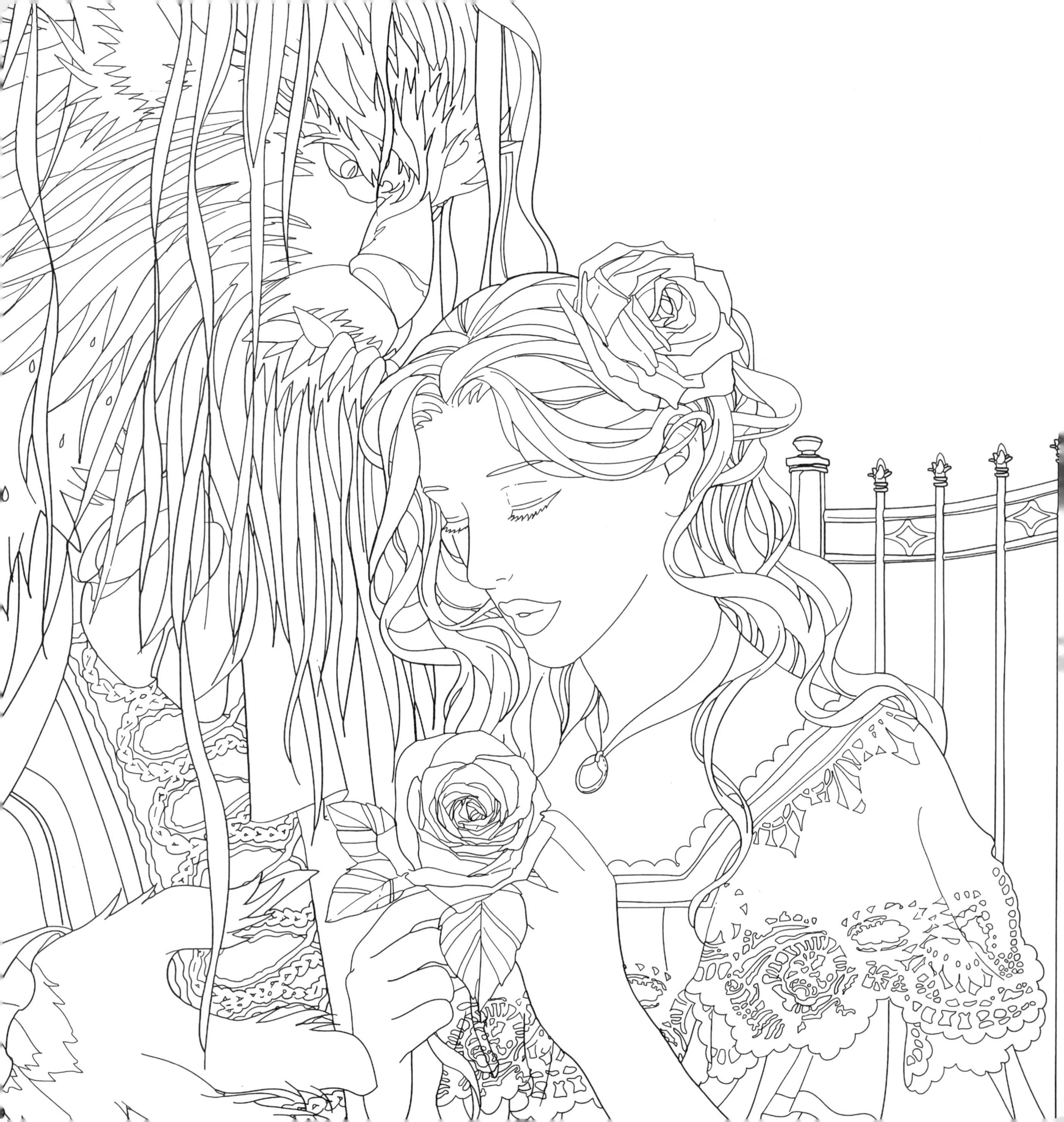

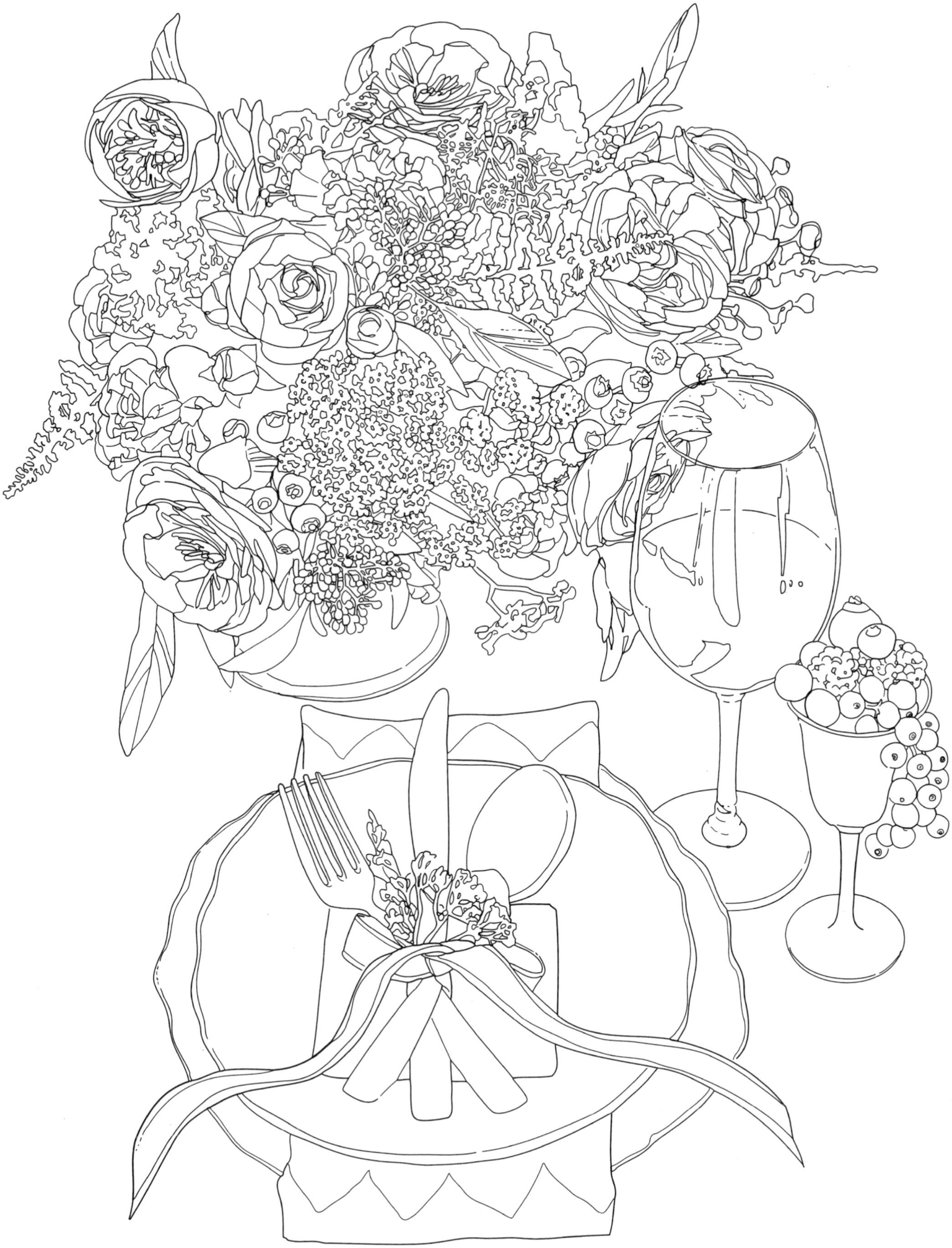

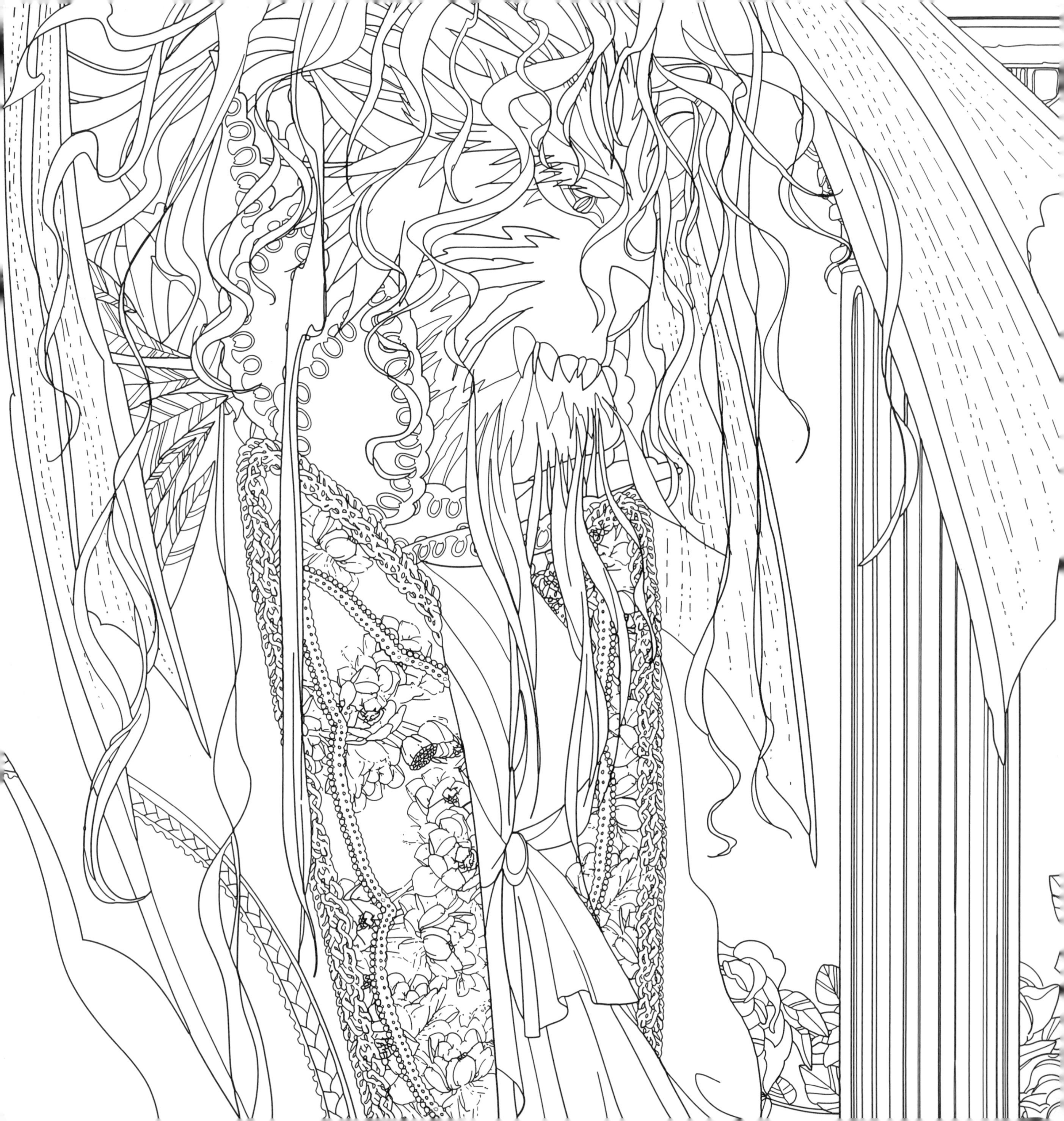

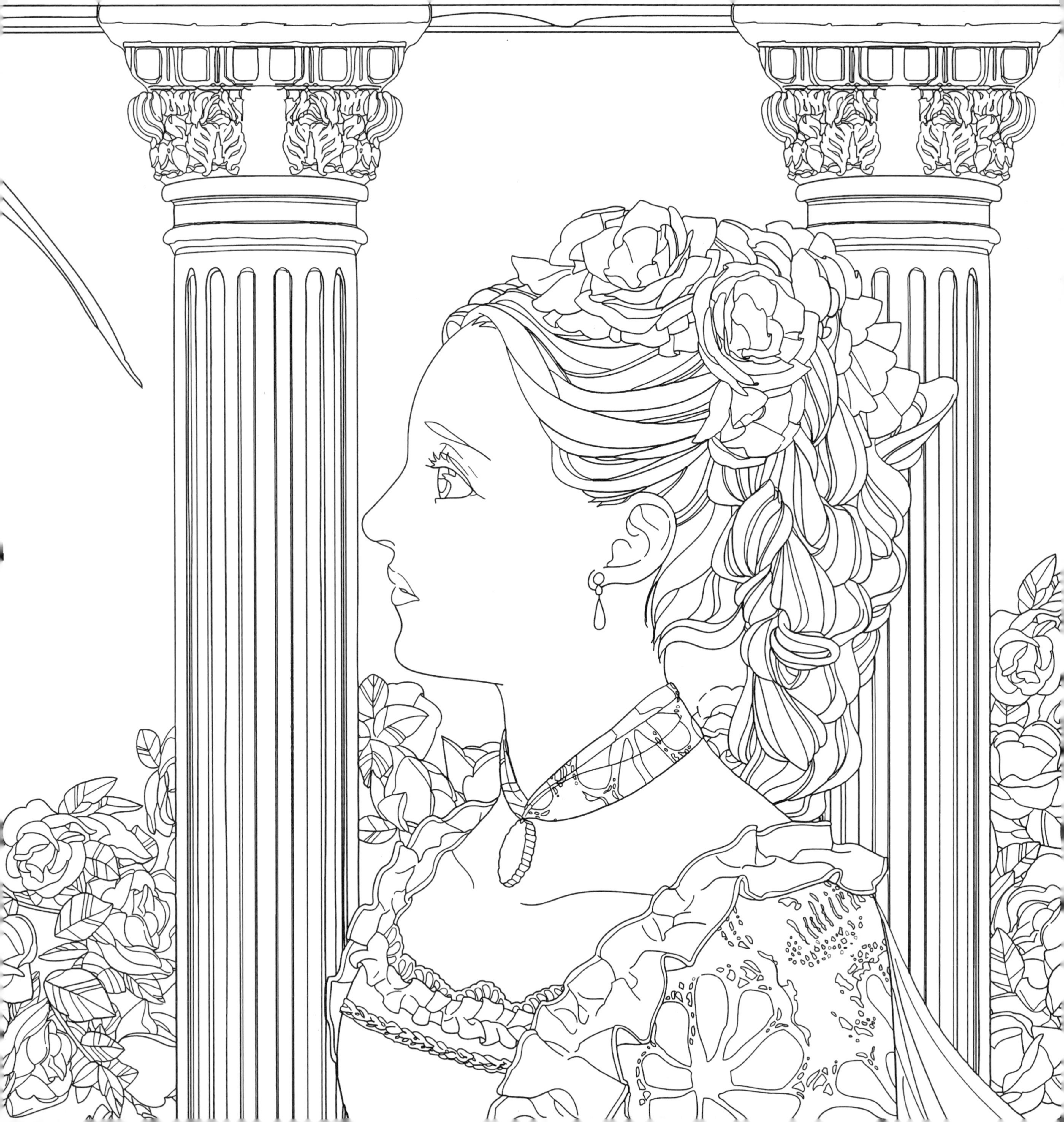

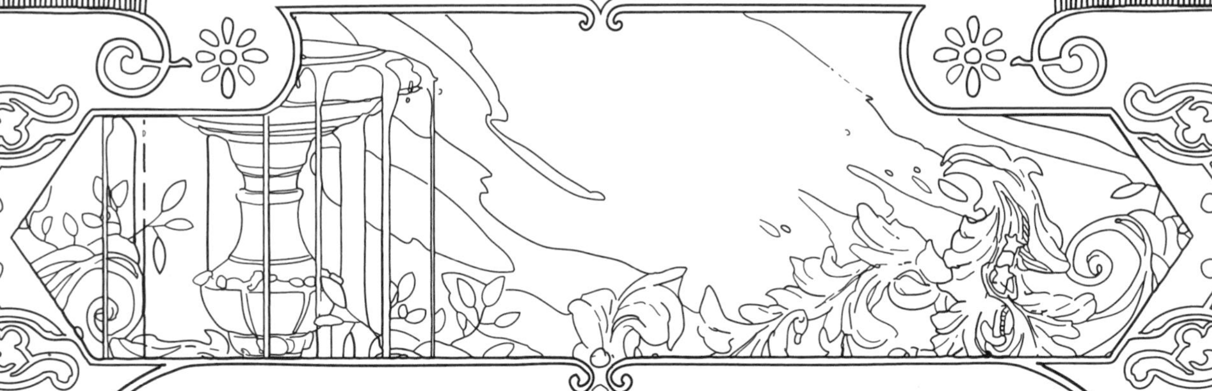

"I would promise without hesitation never to leave you," said Beauty to him, "but I do so long to see my father again, that I shall die of sorrow if you refuse me this pleasure."

"I would rather die myself," said the monster, "than give you pain; I will send you home to your father, you will stay there, and your poor Beast will die of grief at your absence."

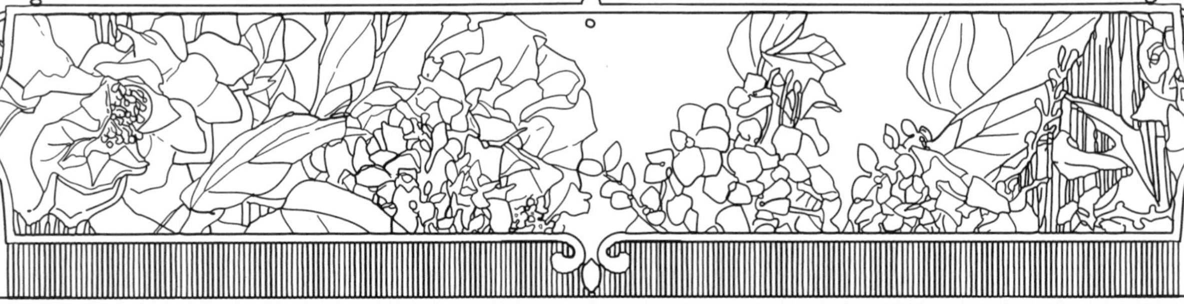

When she awoke the following morning, she found herself at home, and ringing a little bell that stood beside her bed, the maid-servant came in, who gave a loud cry of astonishment at seeing her there. Her father ran in on hearing the cry, and almost died of joy when he found his dear daughter.

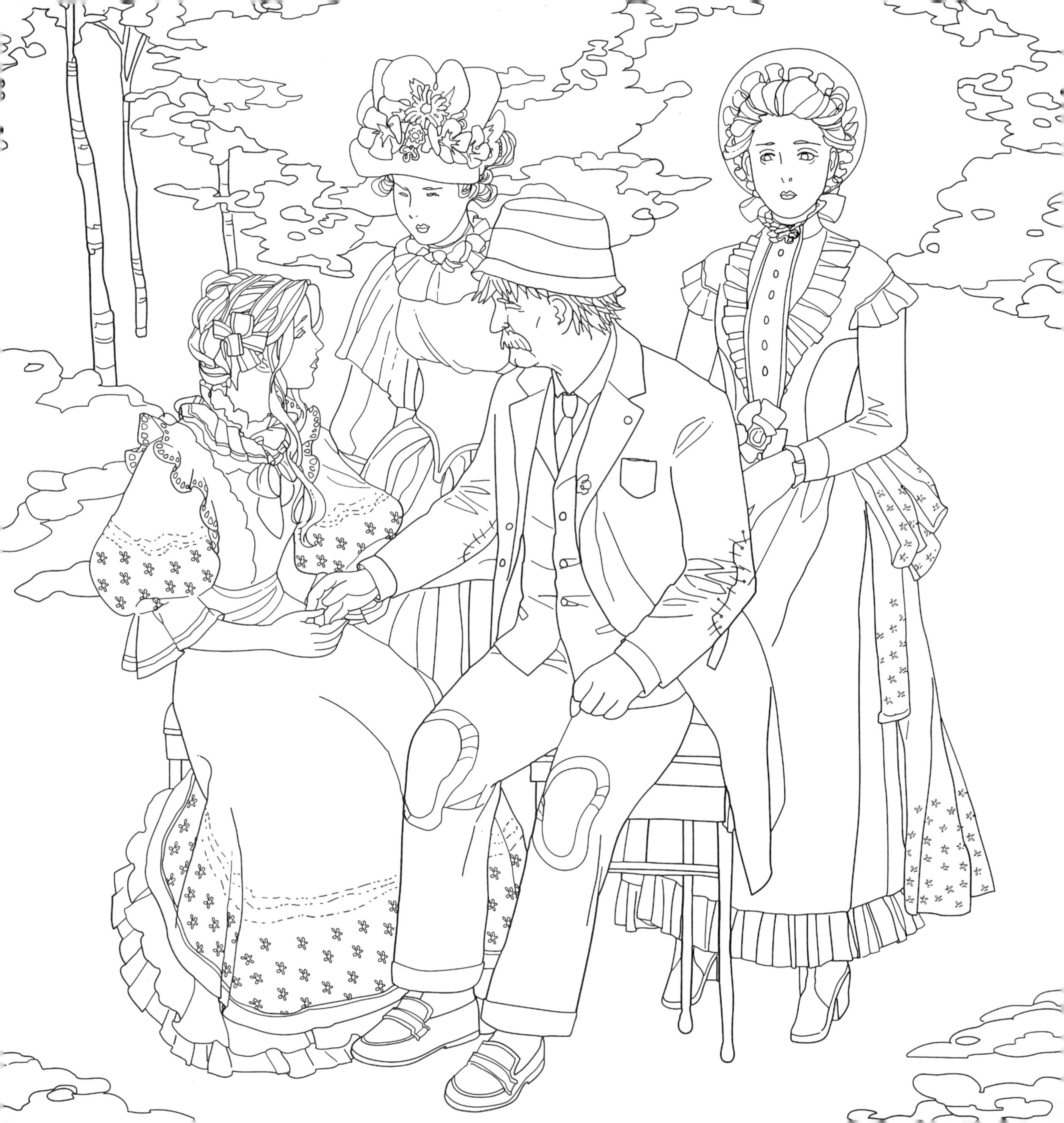

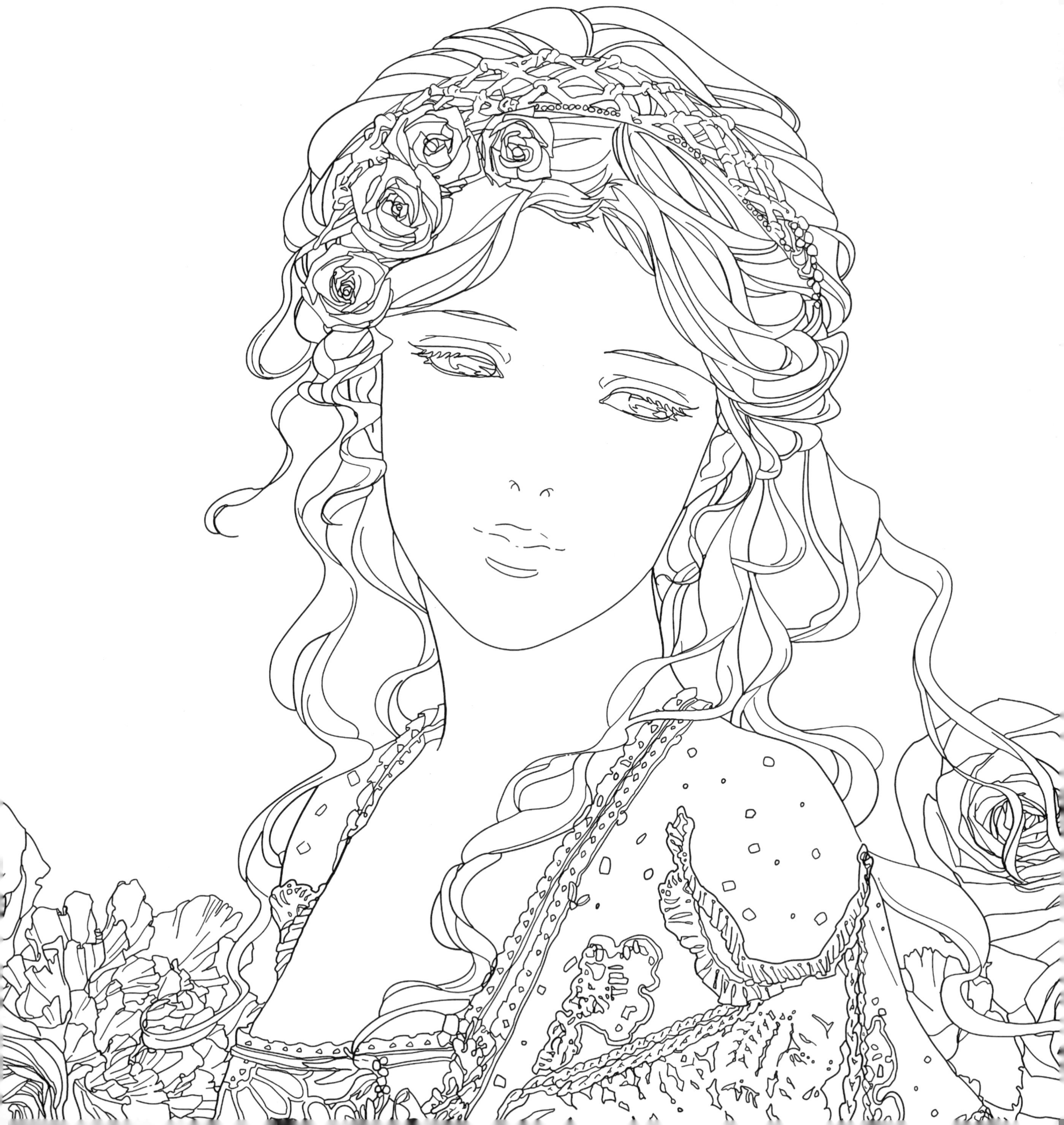

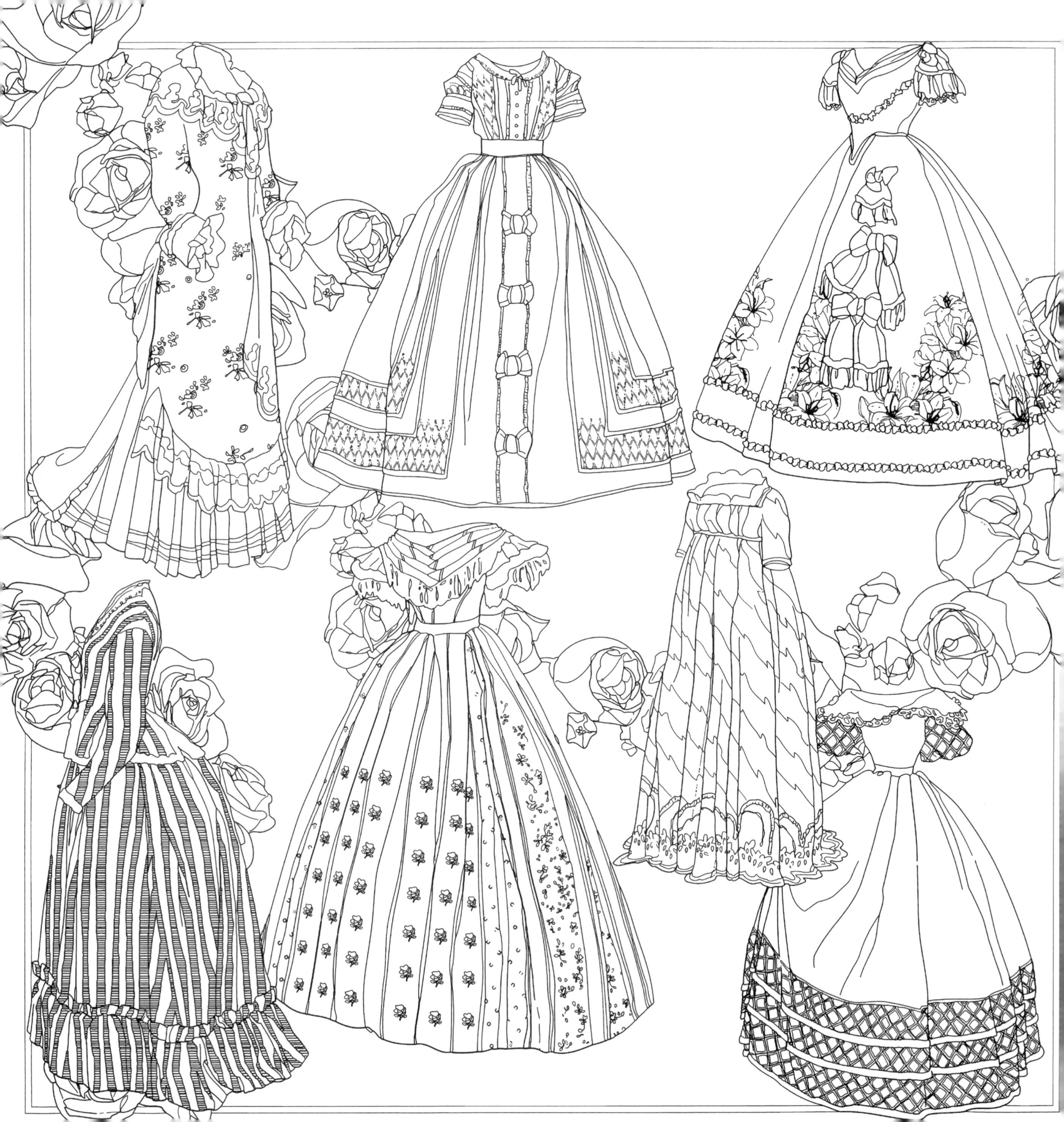

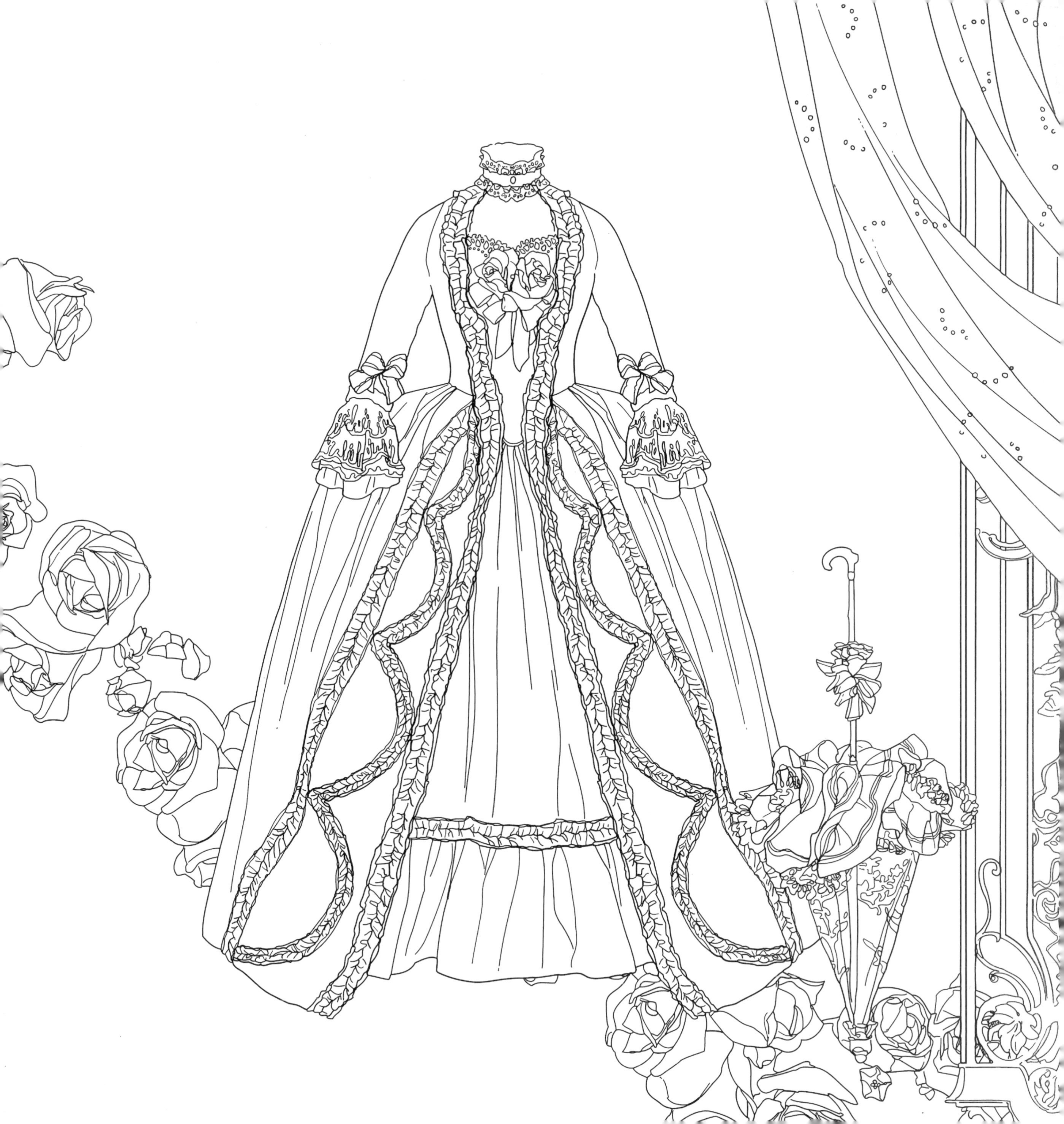

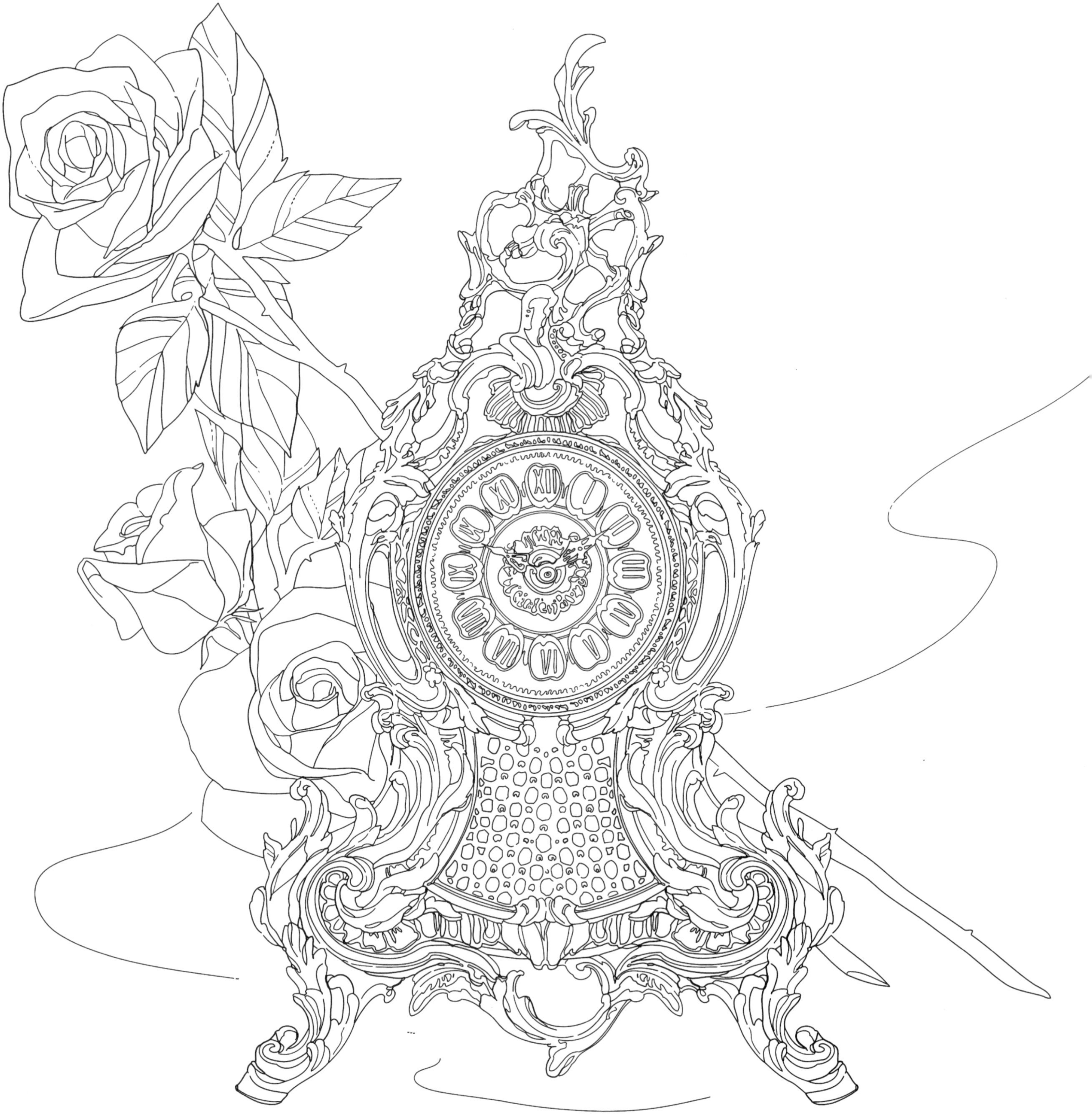

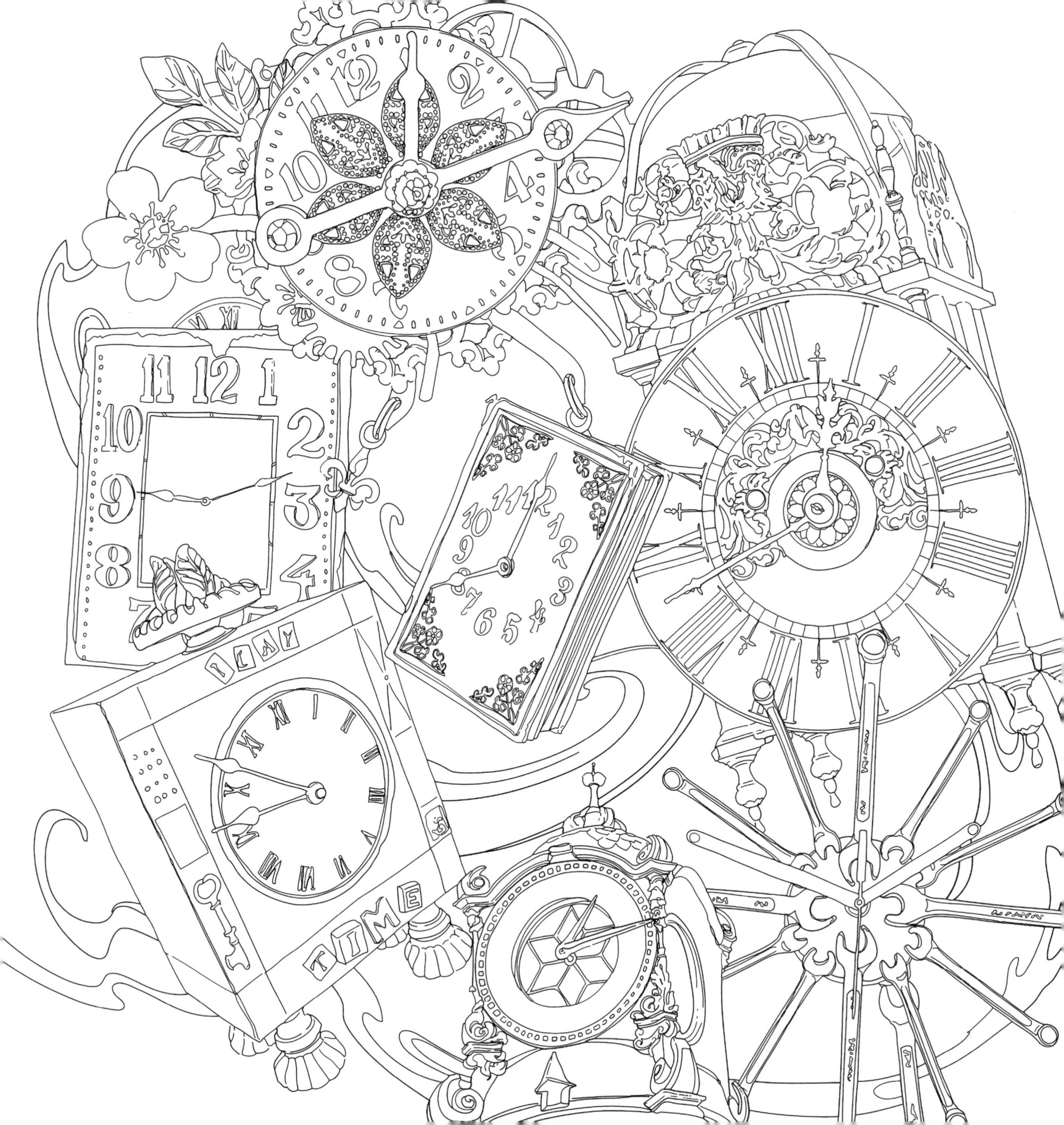
TIME

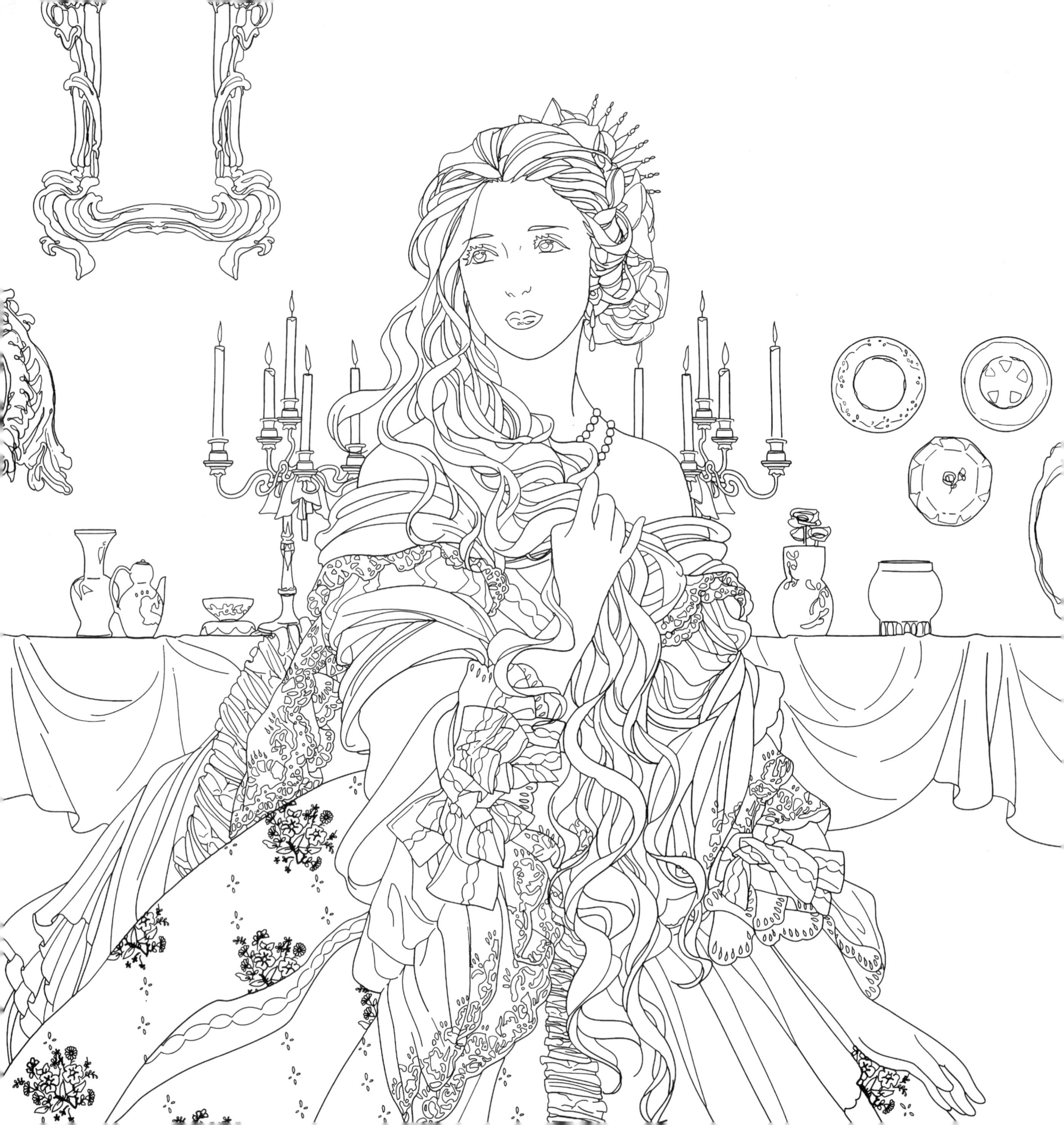

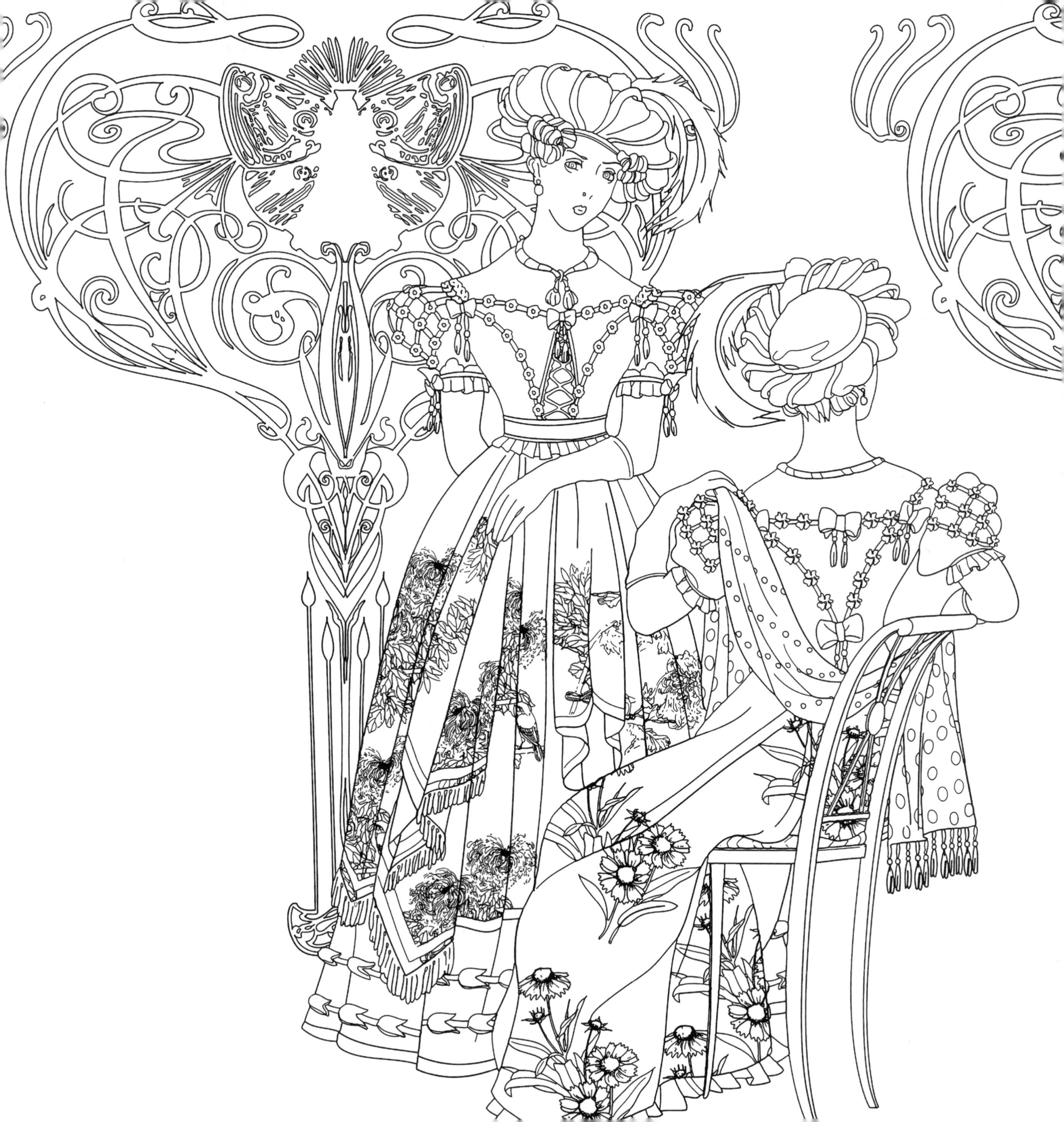

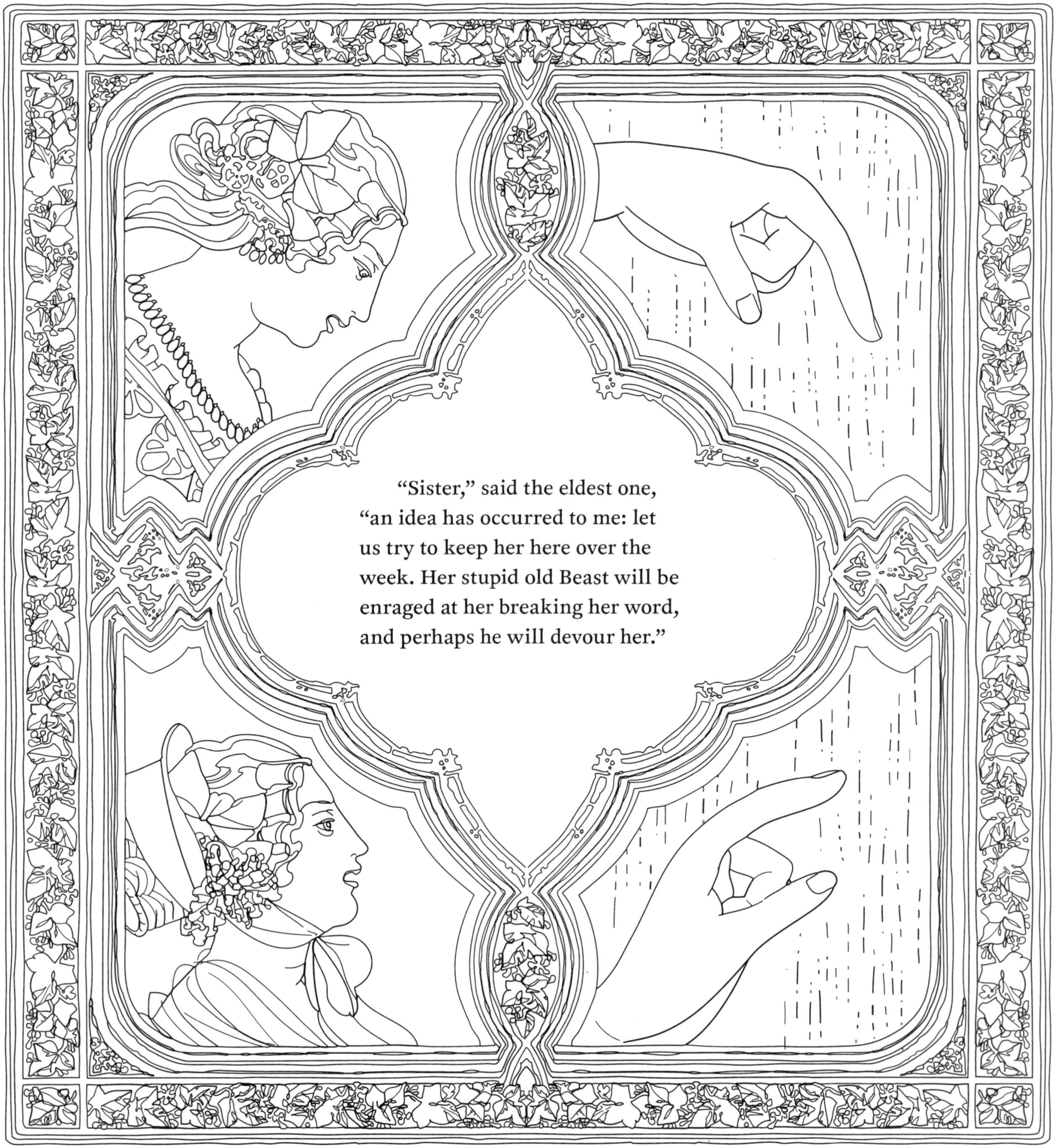

"Sister," said the eldest one, "an idea has occurred to me: let us try to keep her here over the week. Her stupid old Beast will be enraged at her breaking her word, and perhaps he will devour her."

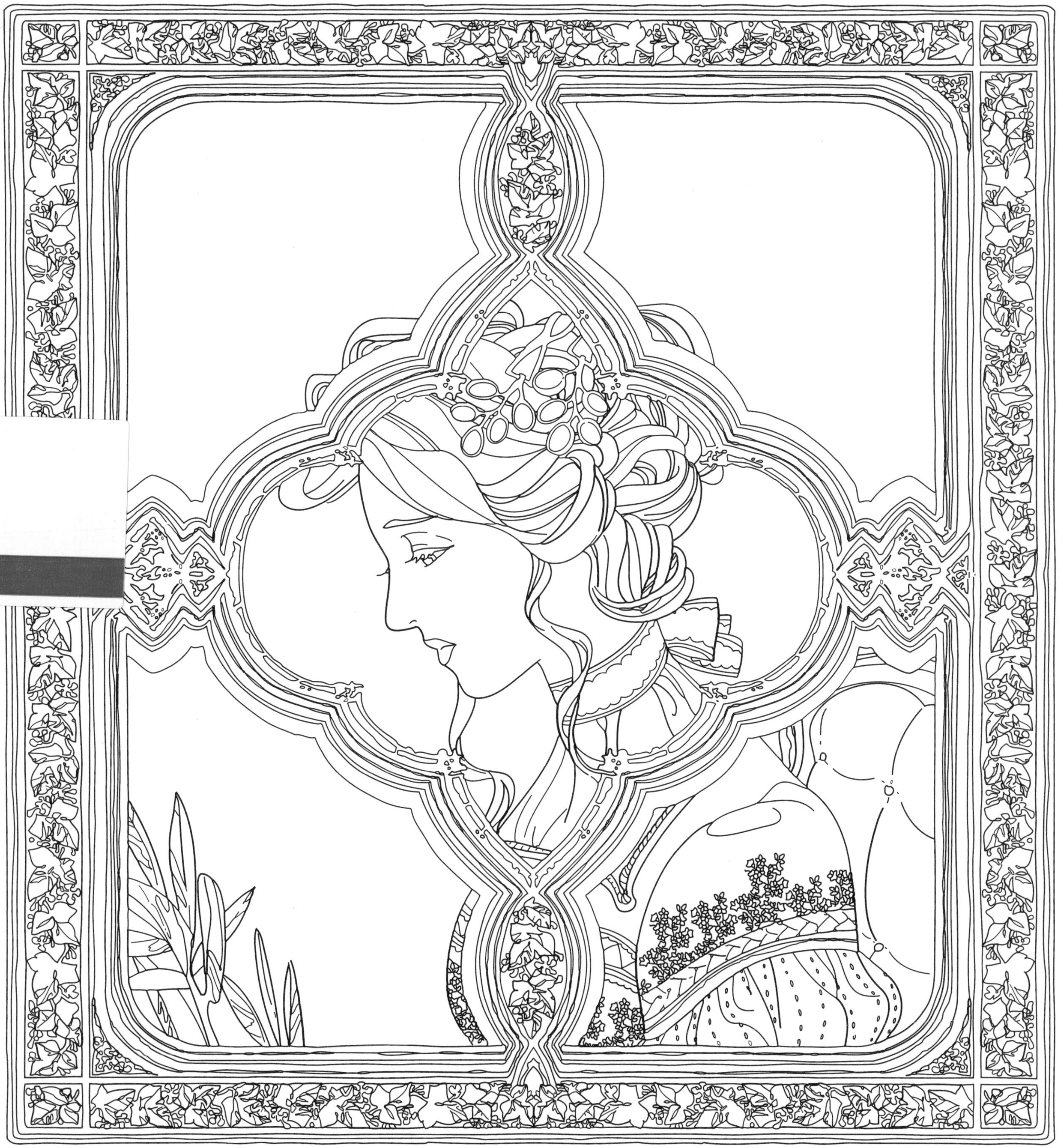

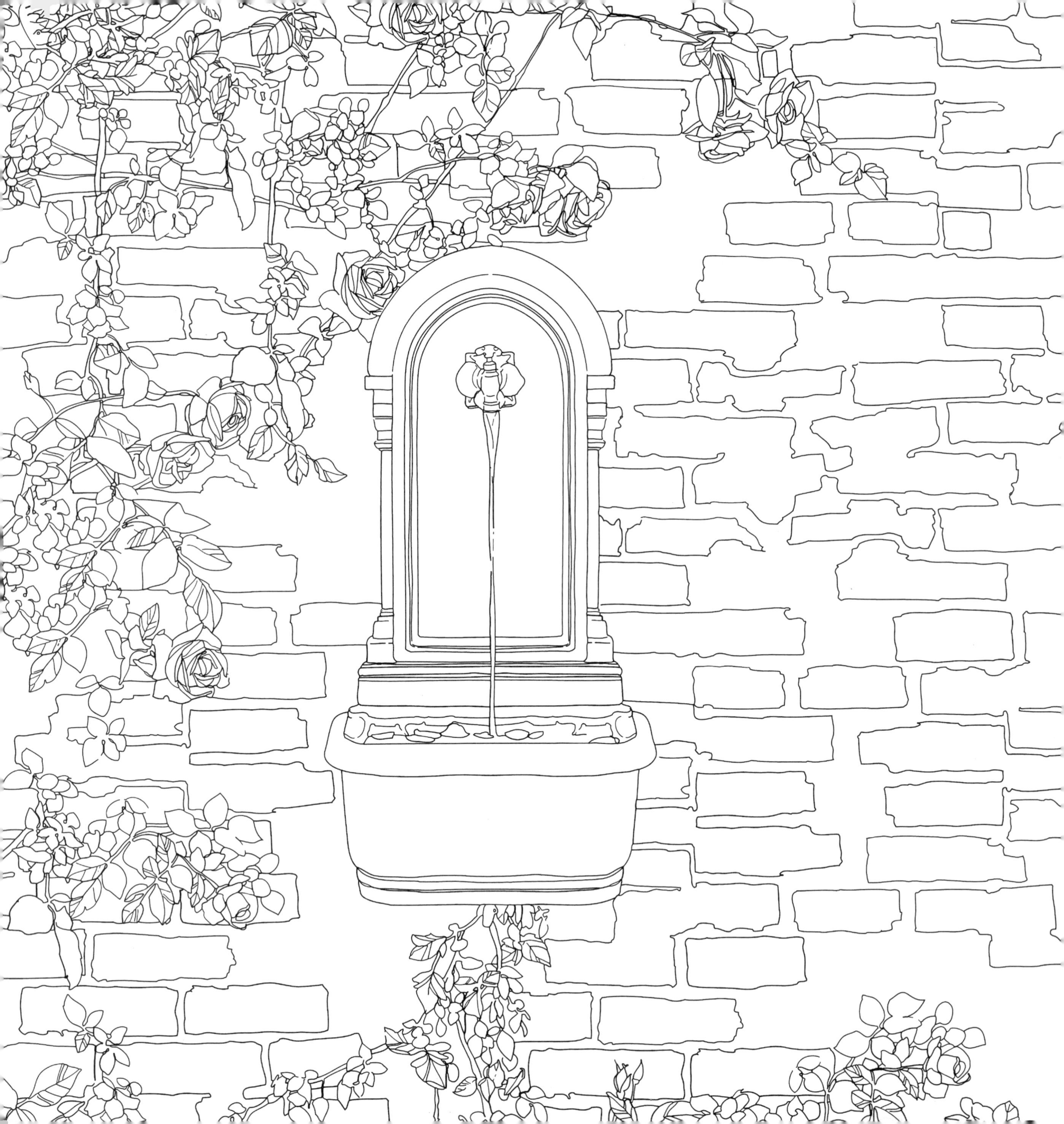

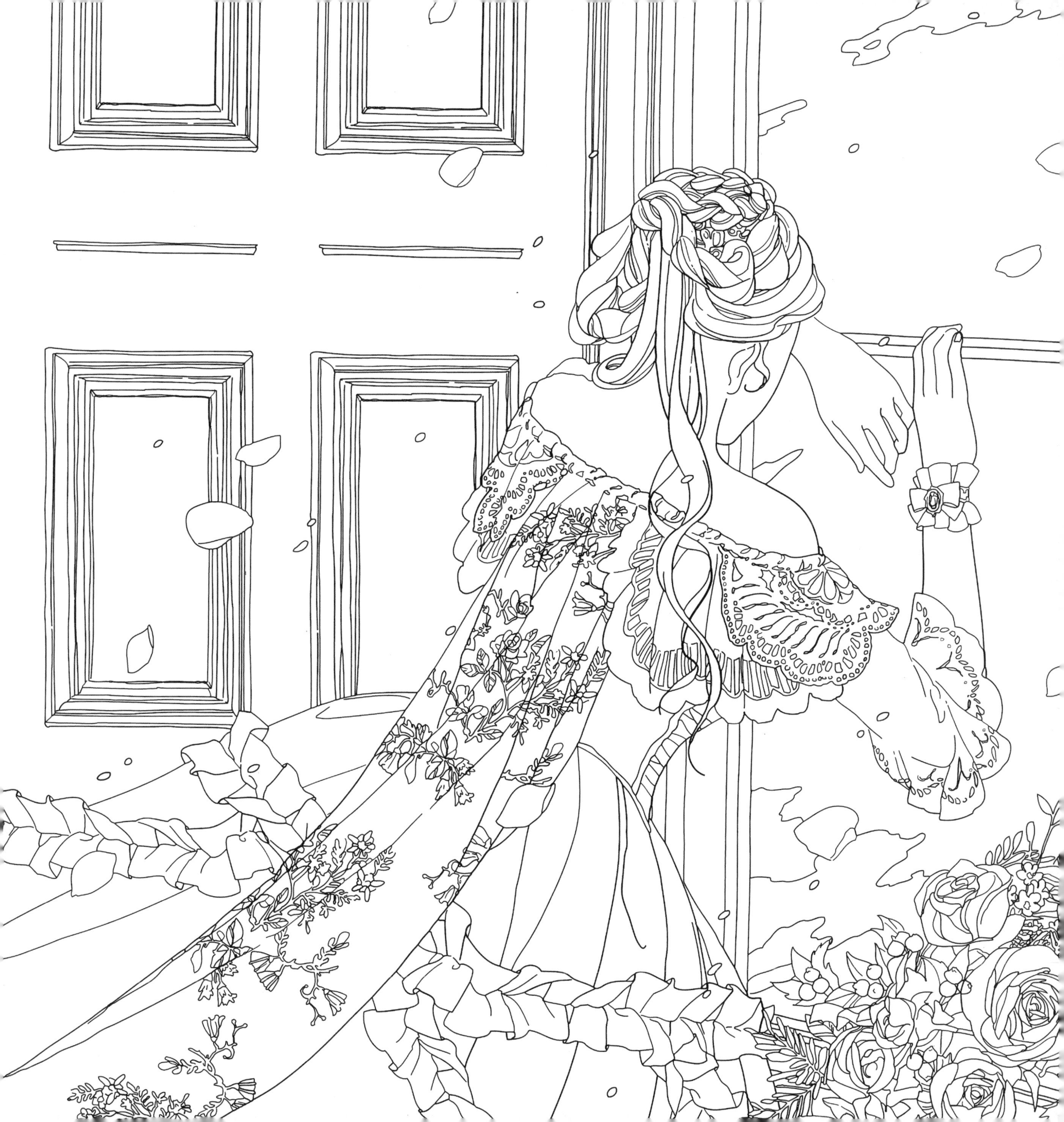

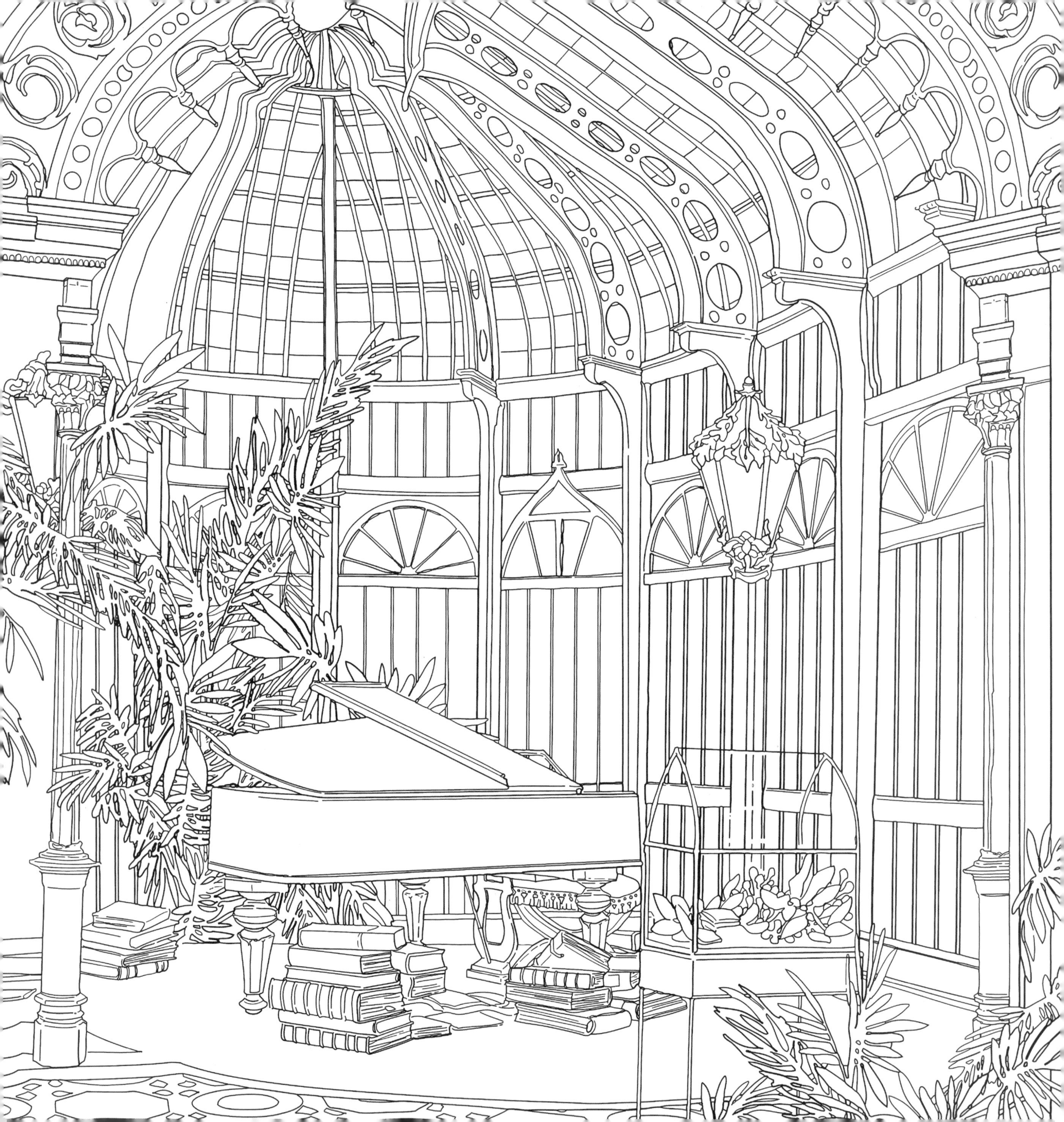

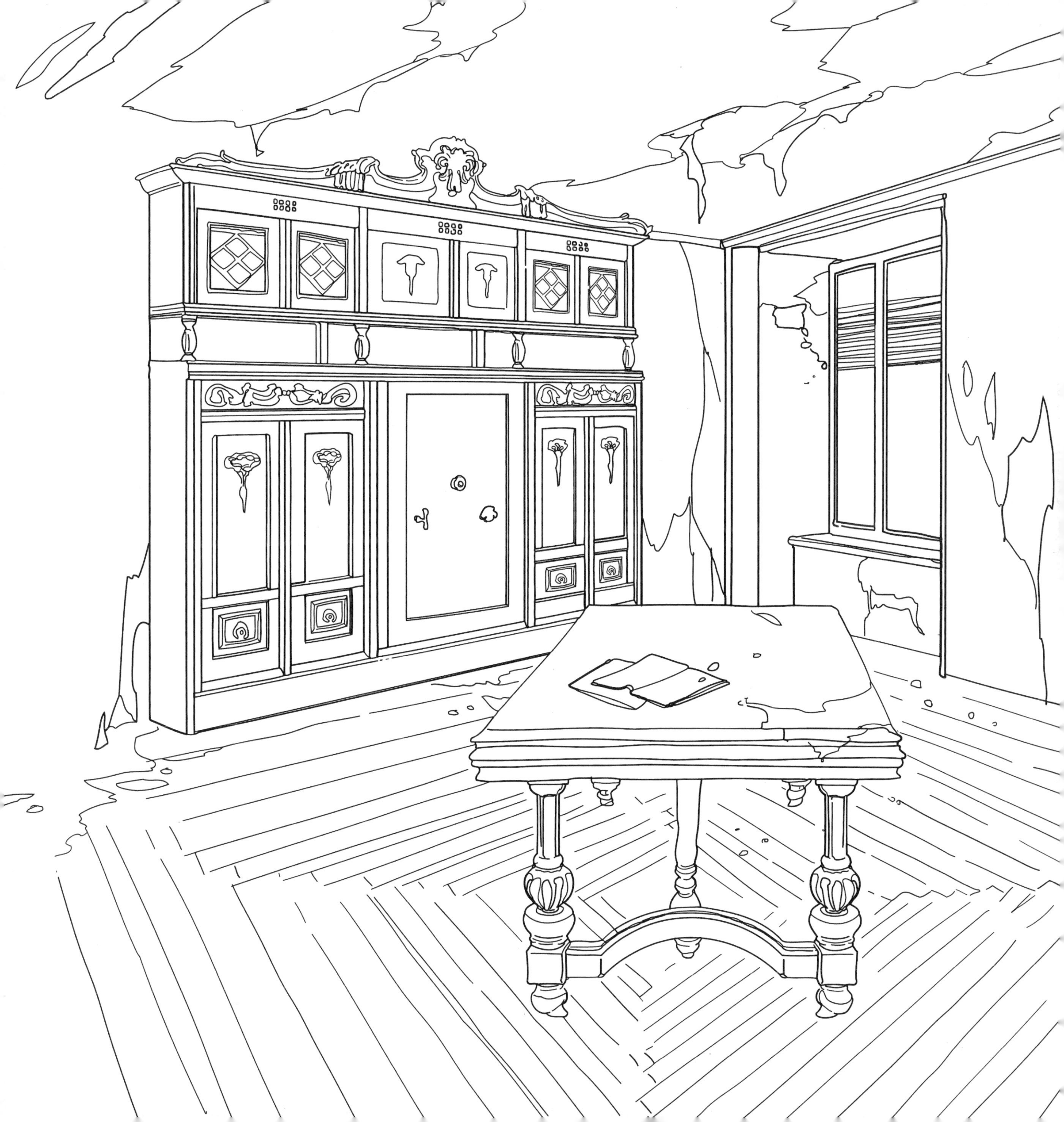

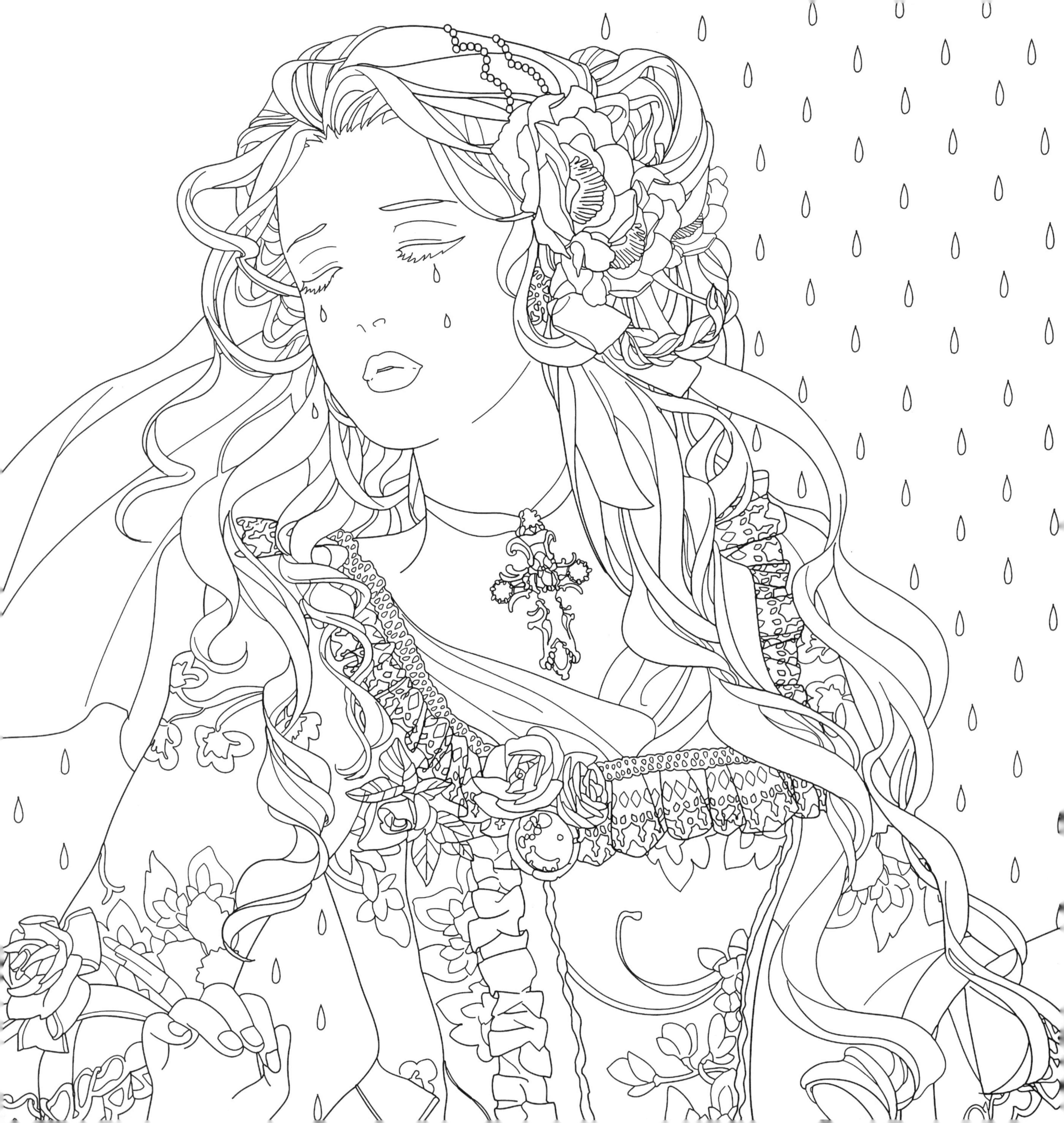

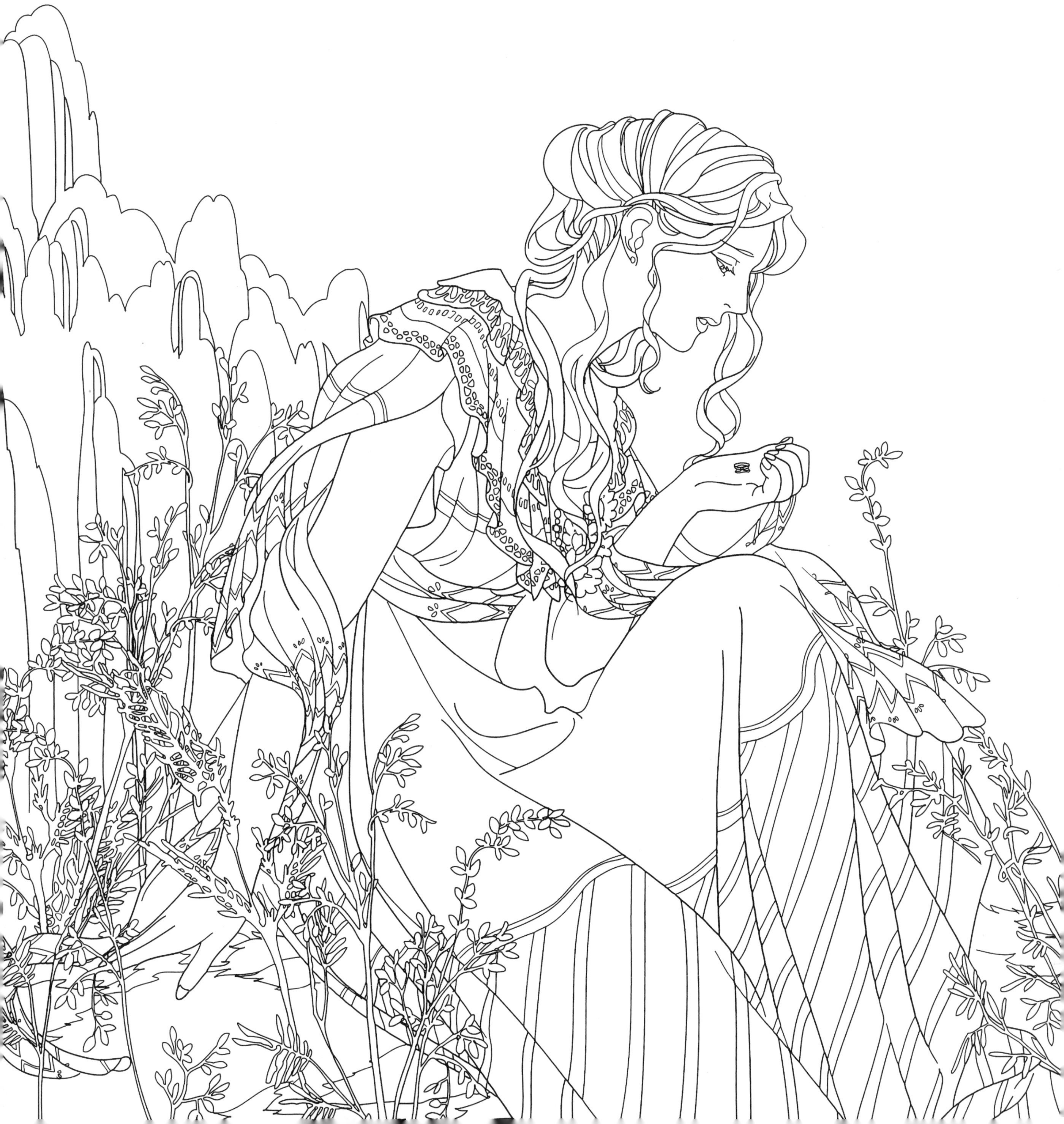

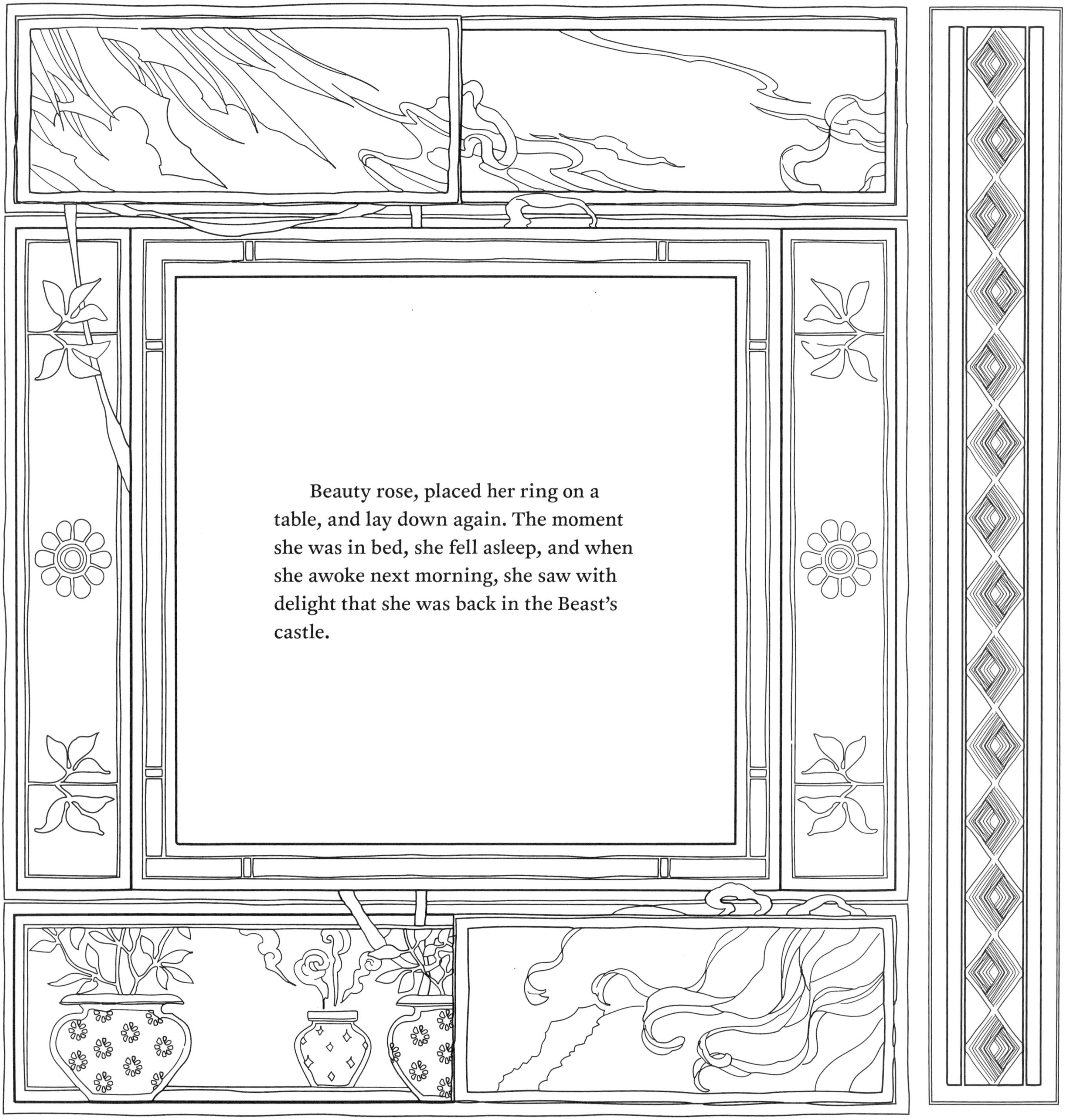

Beauty rose, placed her ring on a table, and lay down again. The moment she was in bed, she fell asleep, and when she awoke next morning, she saw with delight that she was back in the Beast's castle.

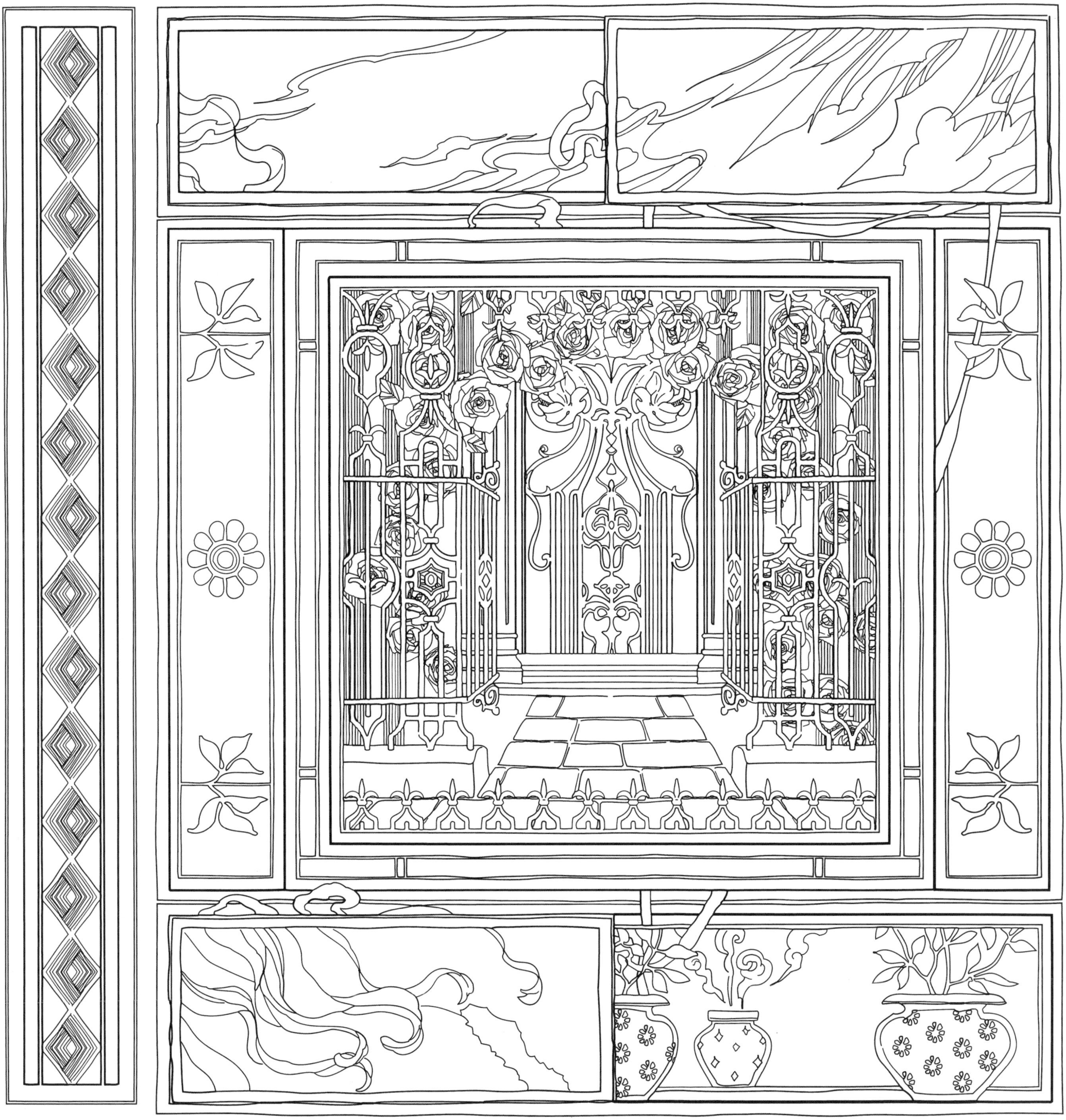

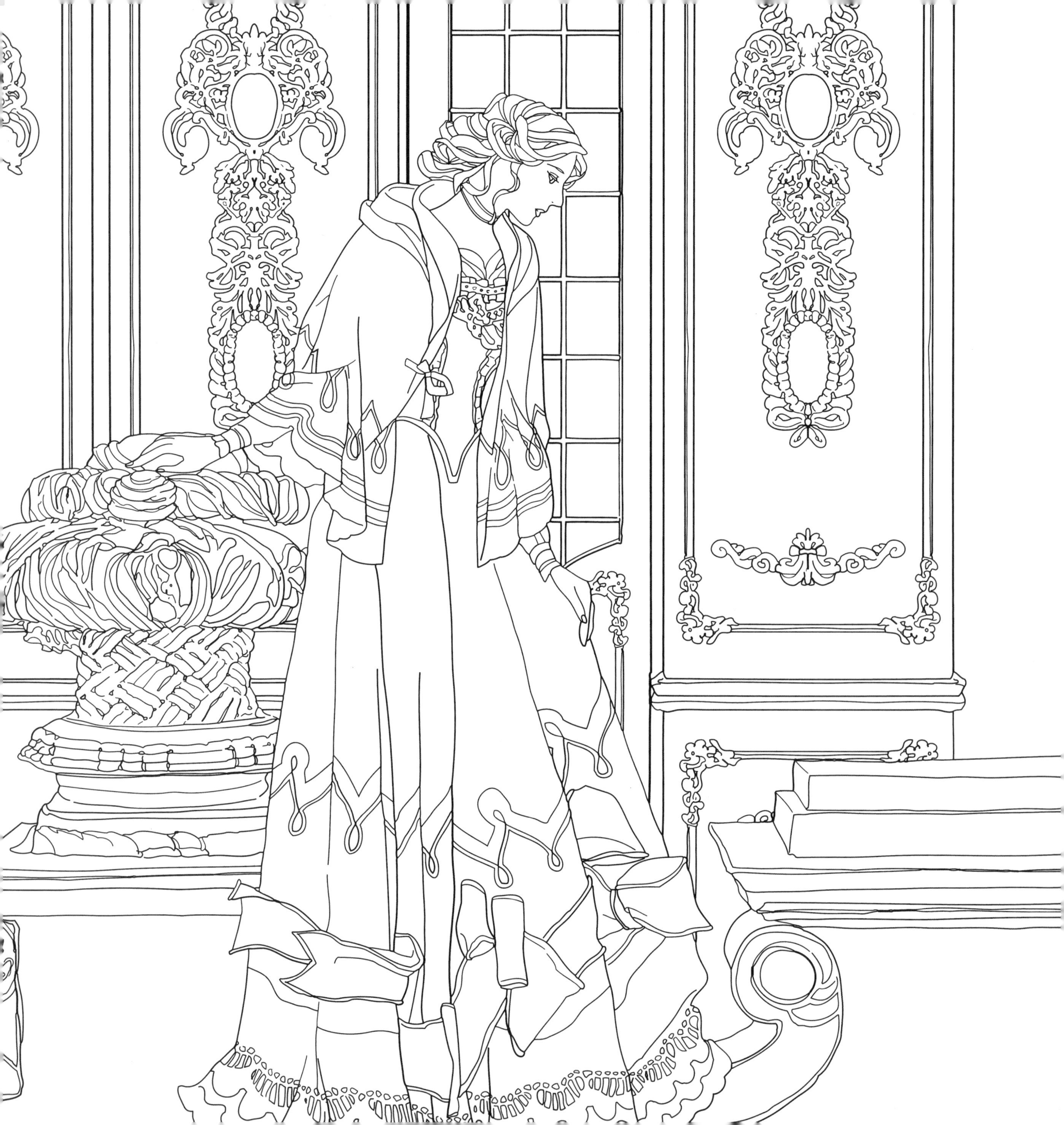

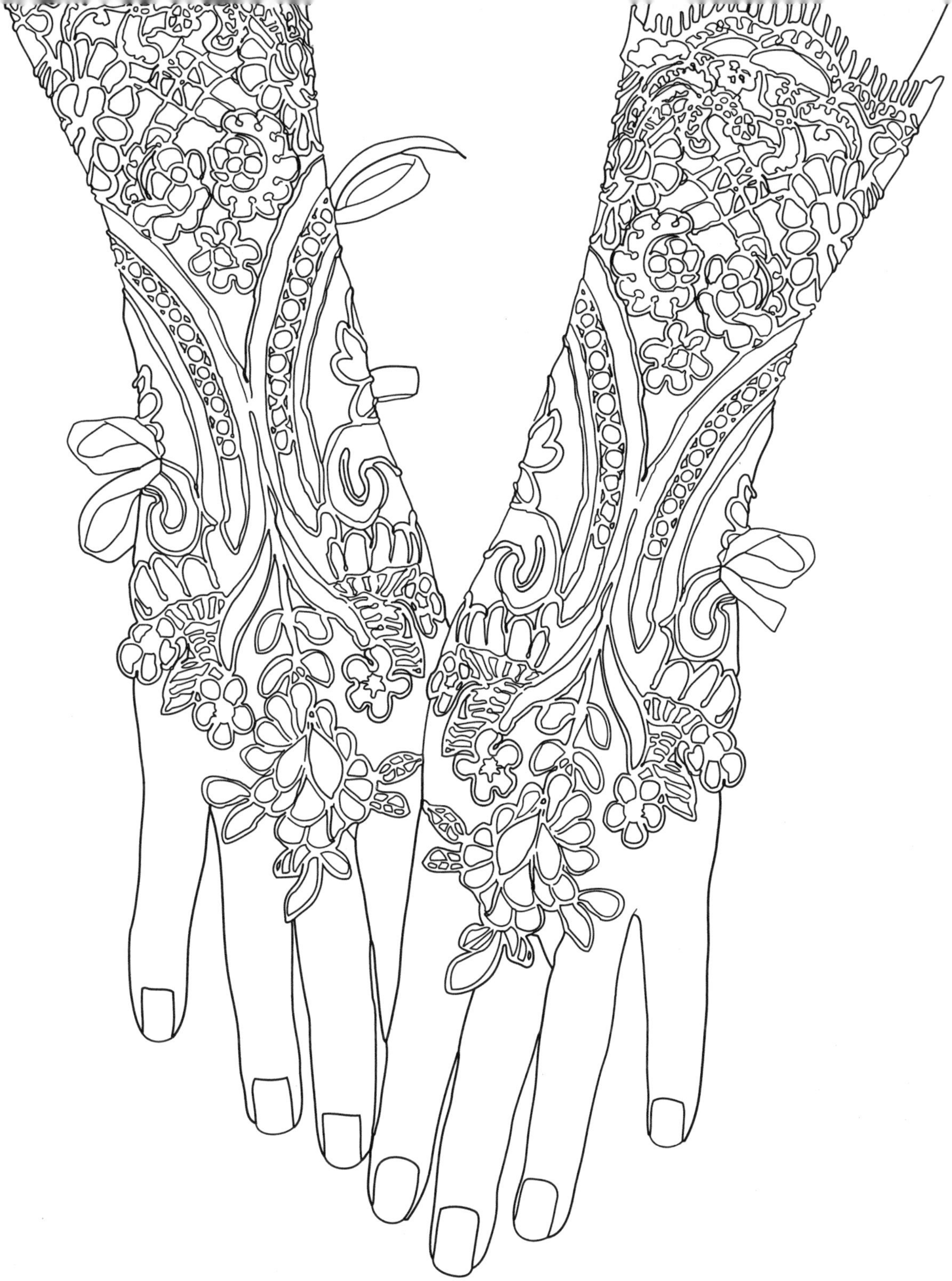

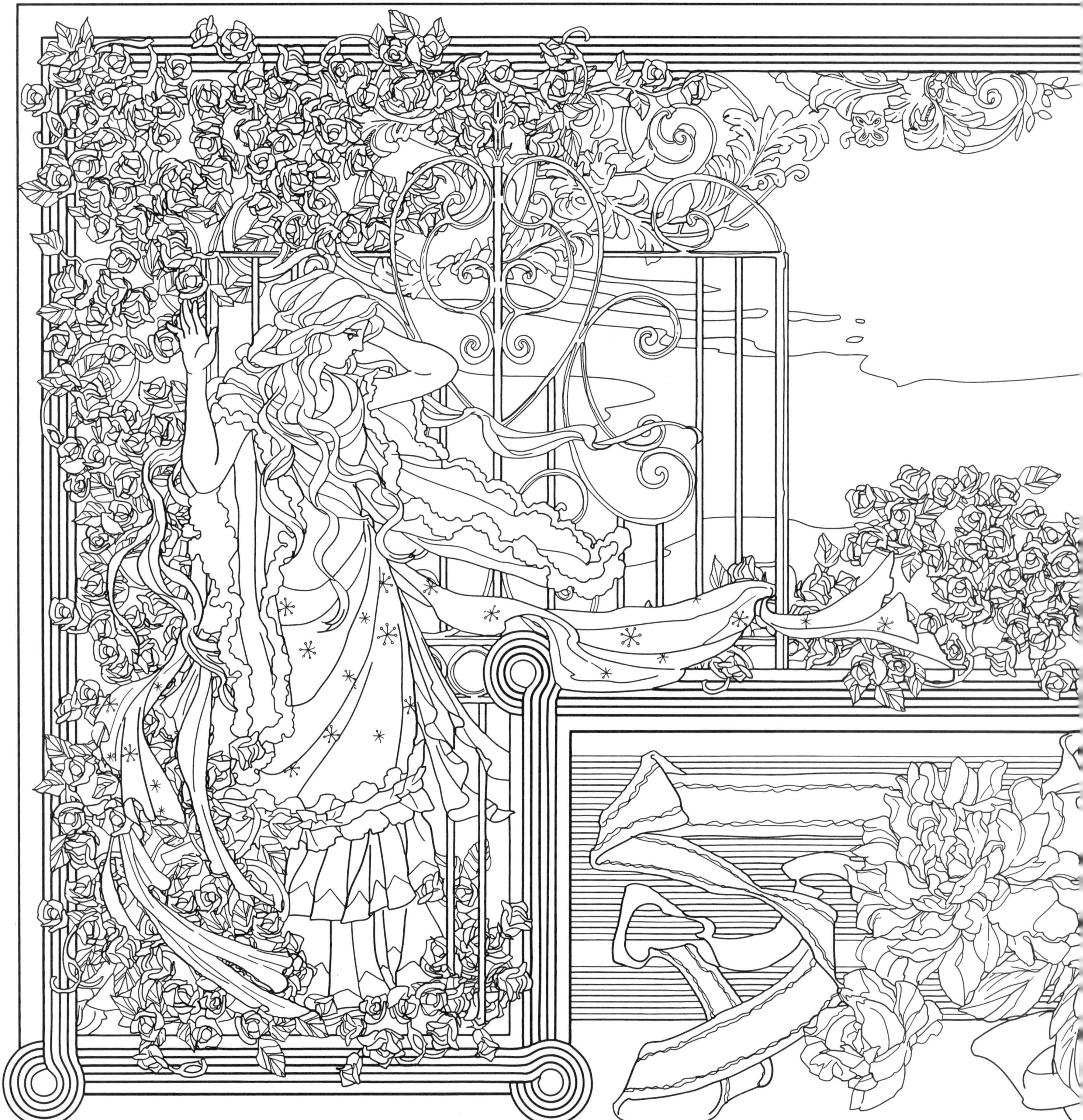

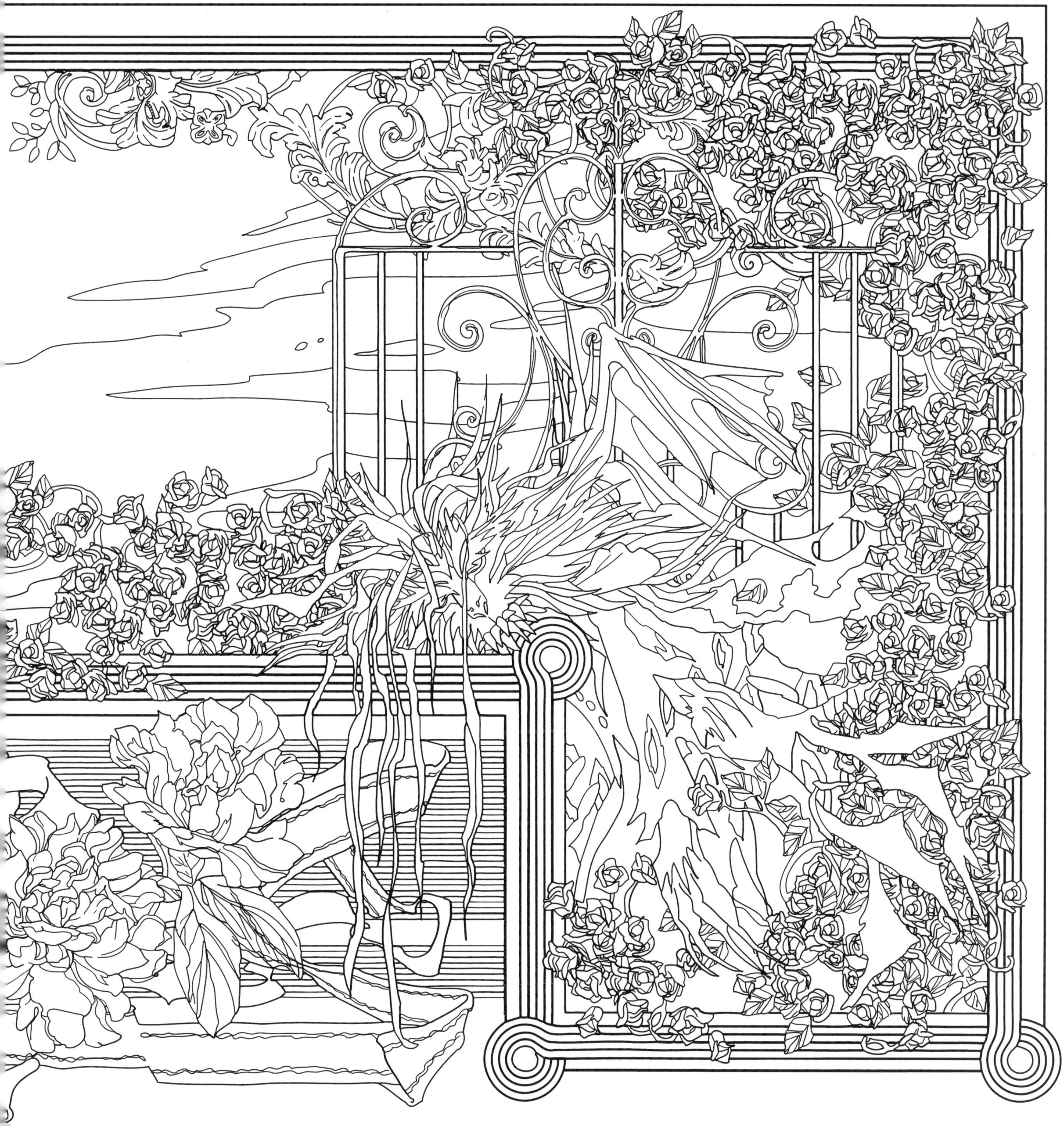

"No, my dear Beast, you shall not die,"
exclaimed Beauty. "You shall live to be my
husband; I am yours from this moment,
and only yours."

Beauty had scarcely uttered these words before she saw the castle suddenly become brilliantly illuminated, while fire-works, music, everything indicated the celebration of some joyful event.

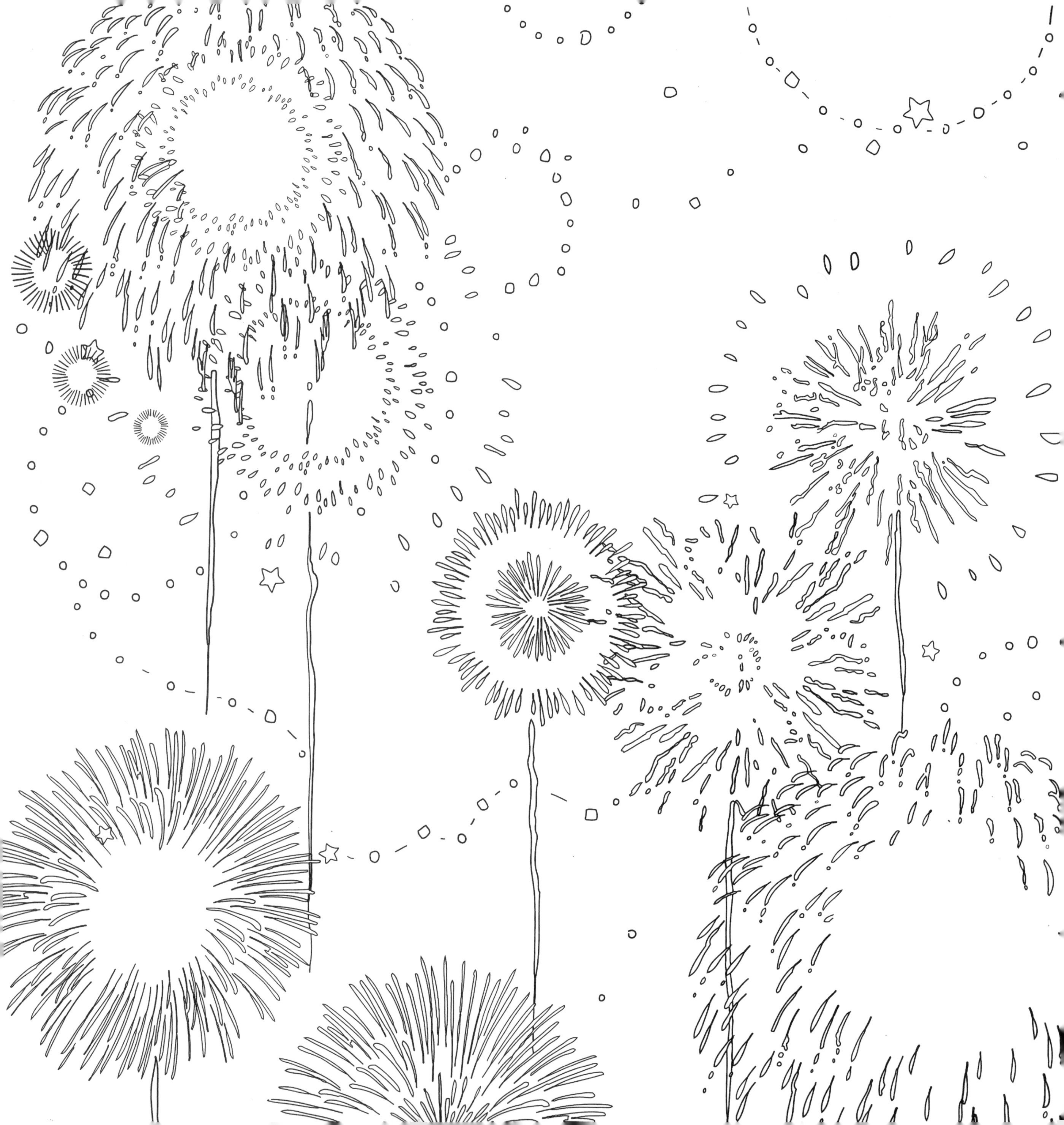

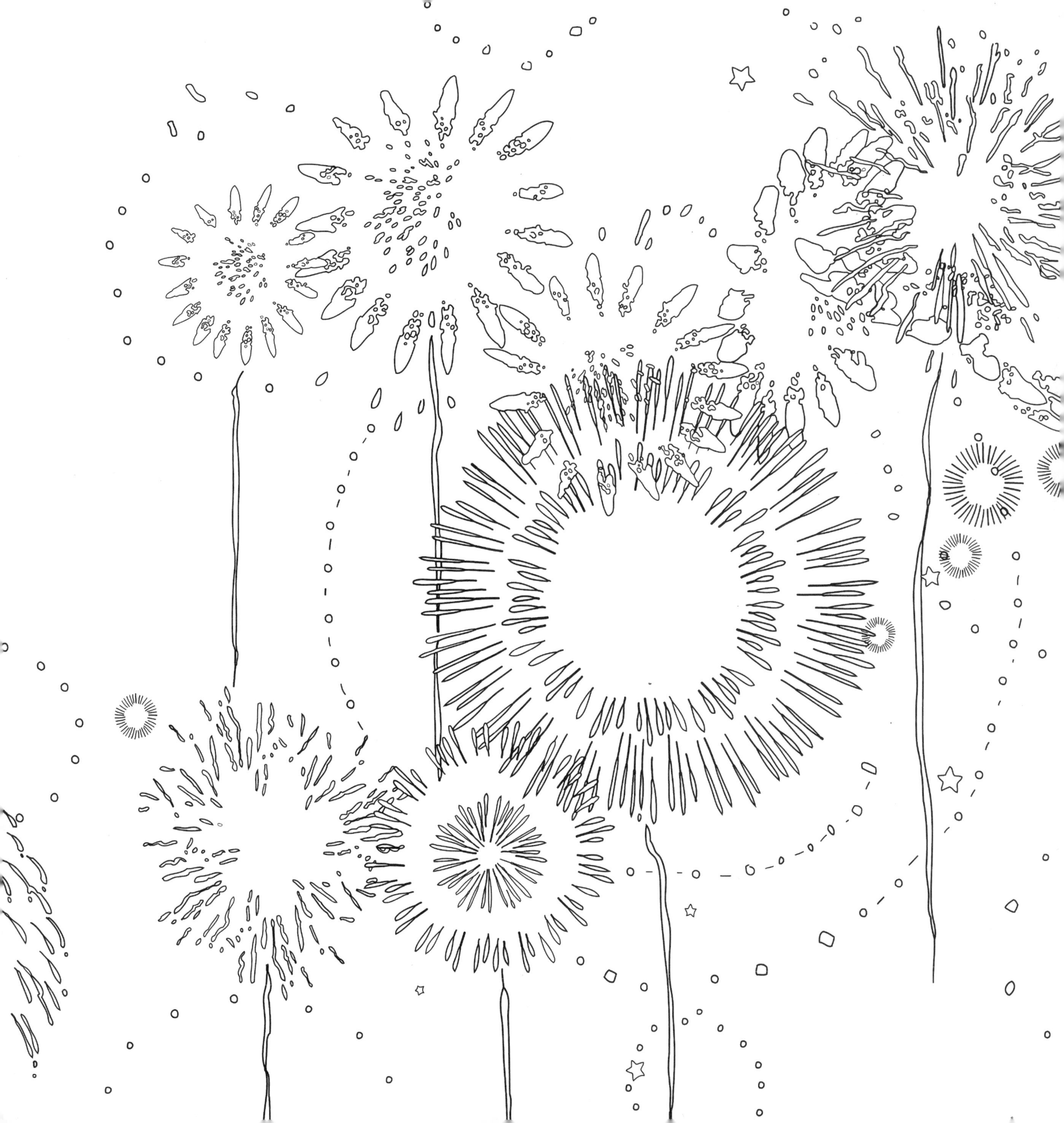

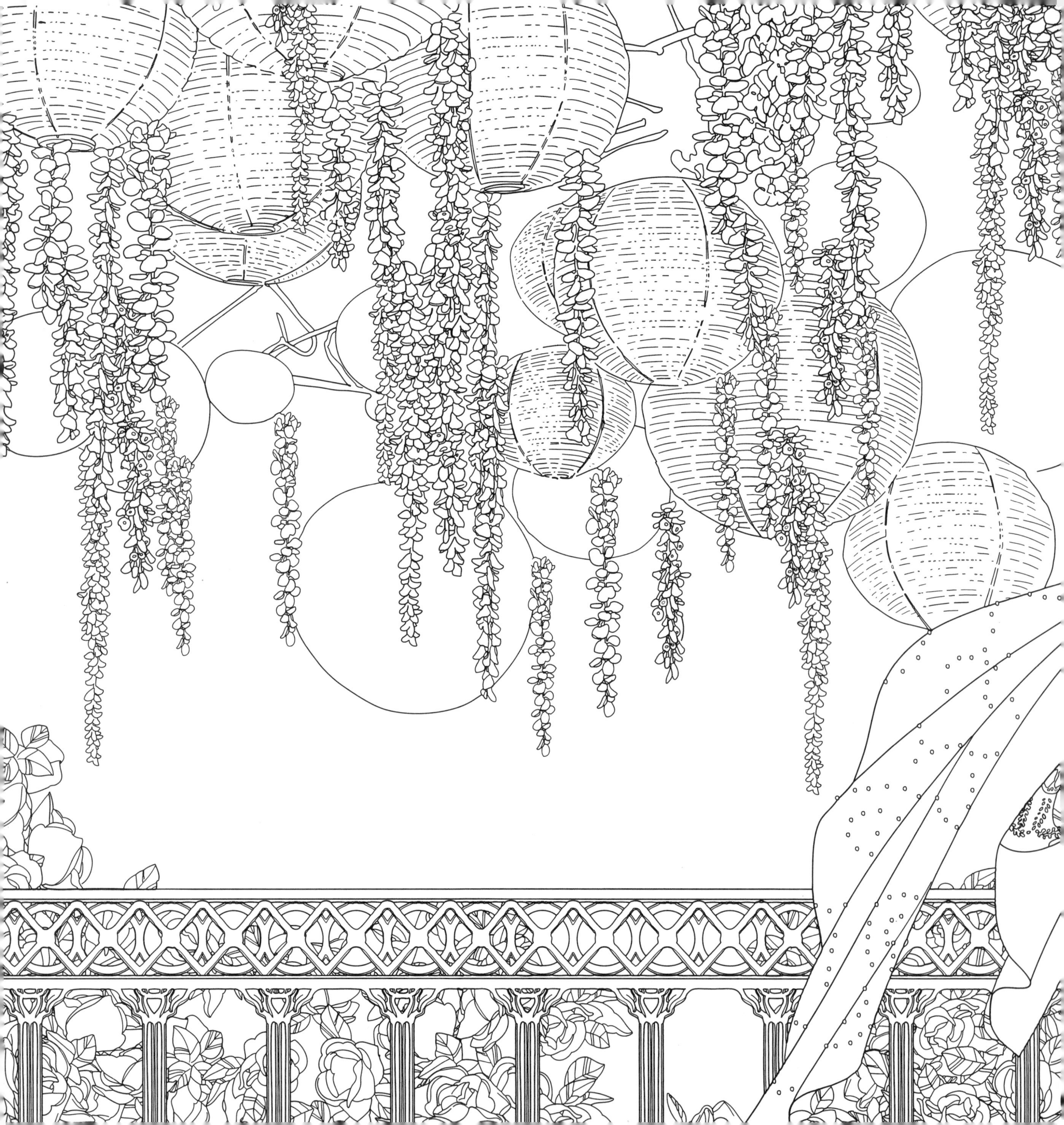

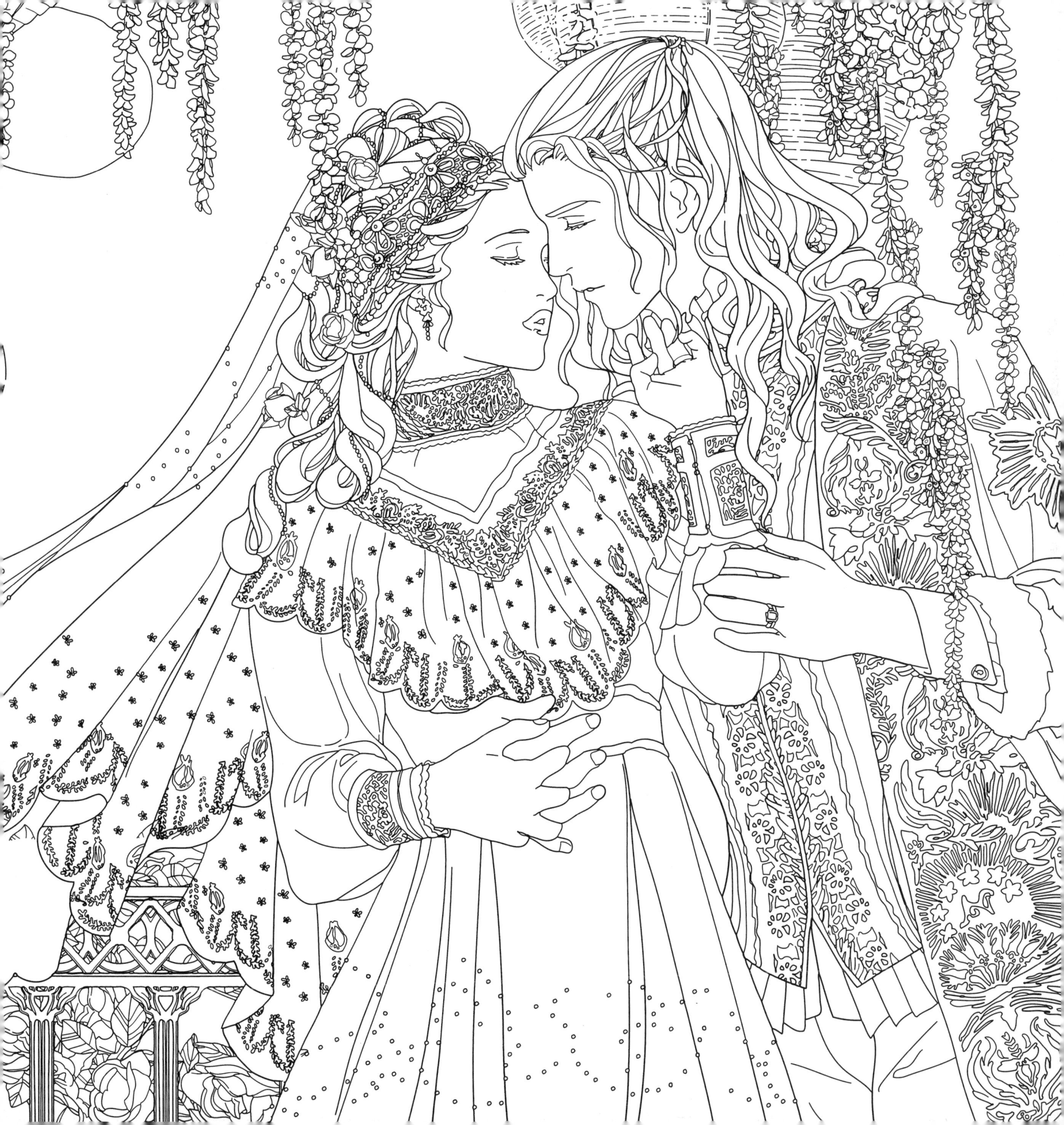

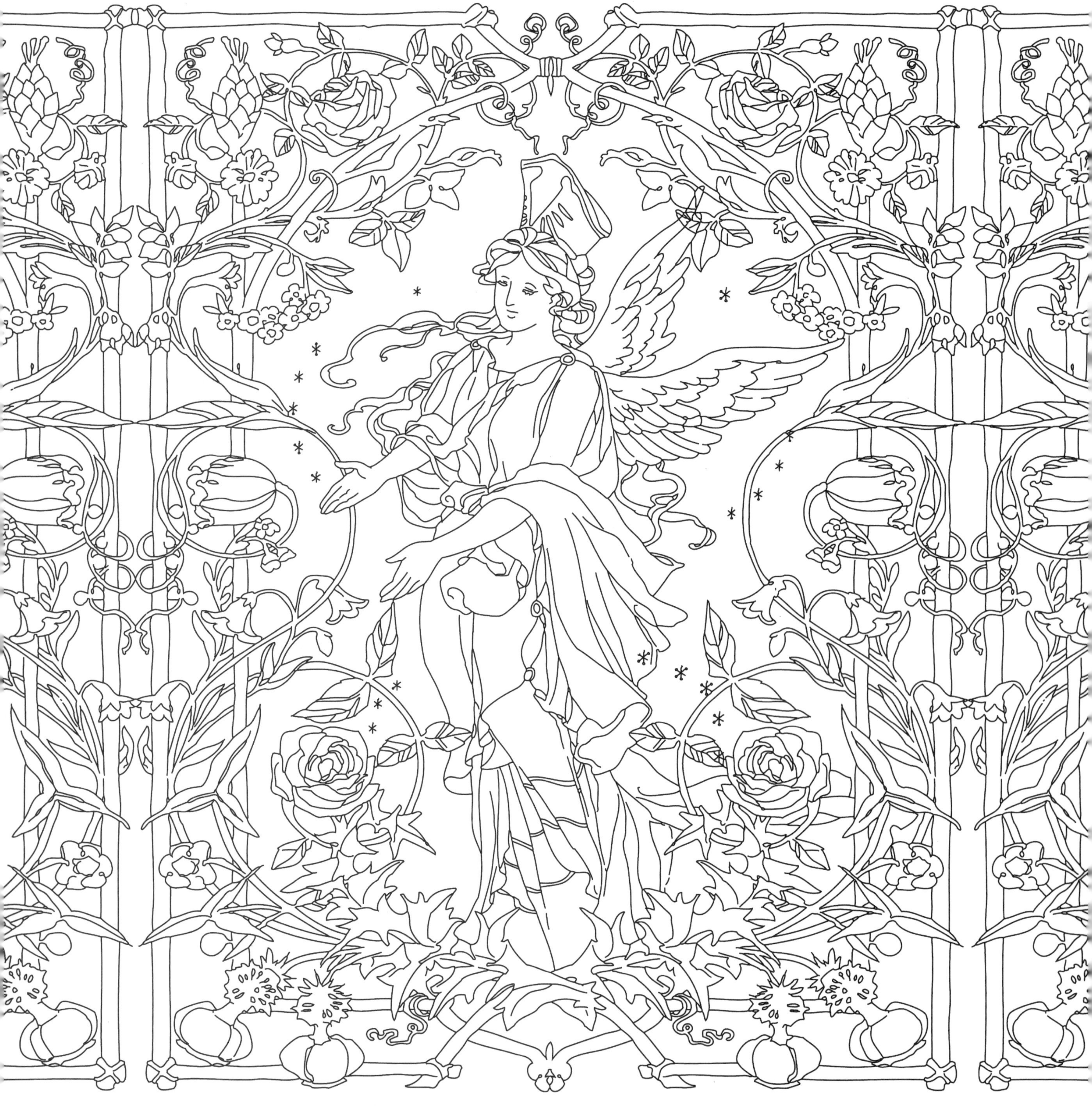

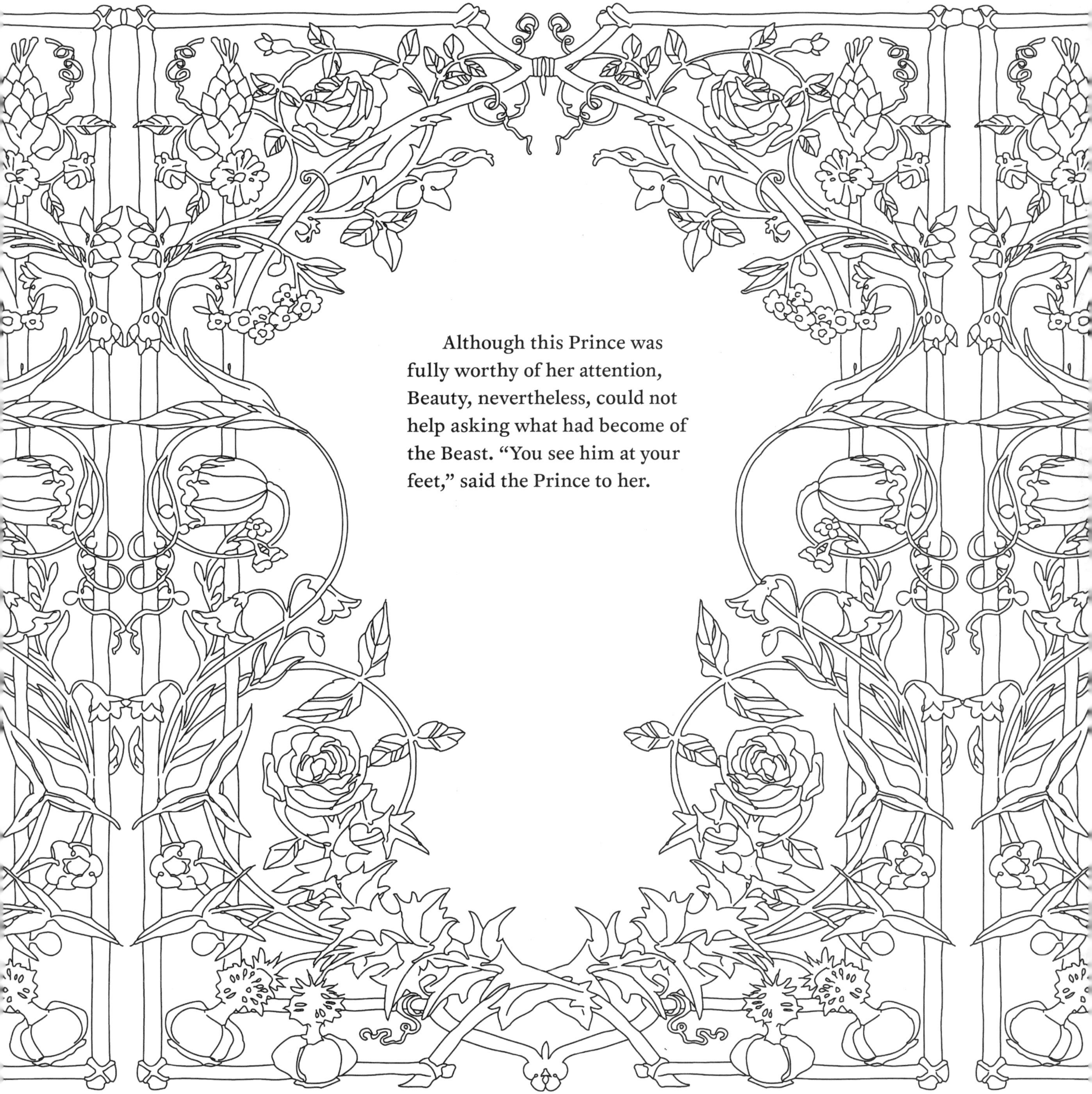

Although this Prince was fully worthy of her attention, Beauty, nevertheless, could not help asking what had become of the Beast. "You see him at your feet," said the Prince to her.

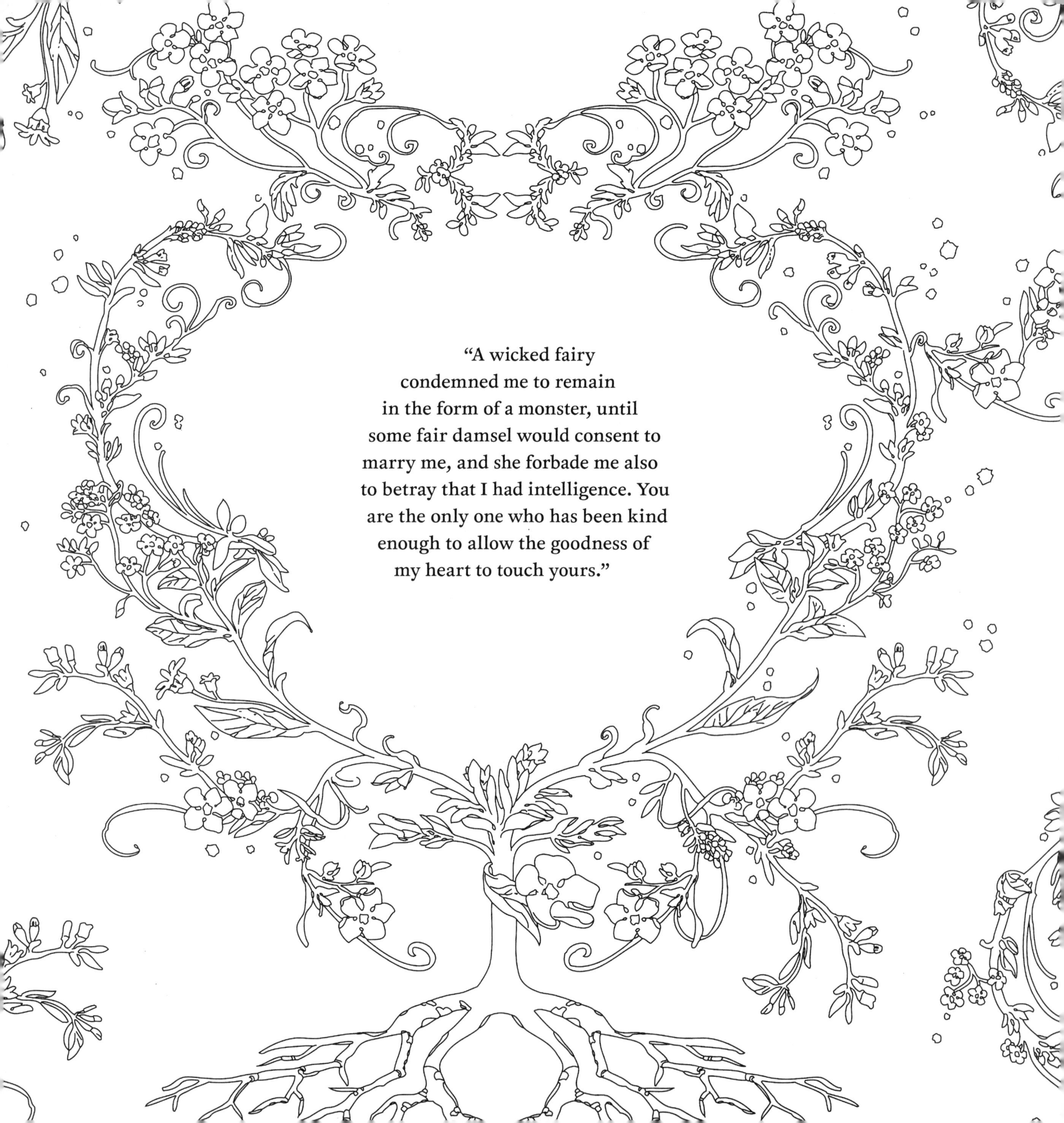

"A wicked fairy
condemned me to remain
in the form of a monster, until
some fair damsel would consent to
marry me, and she forbade me also
to betray that I had intelligence. You
are the only one who has been kind
enough to allow the goodness of
my heart to touch yours."

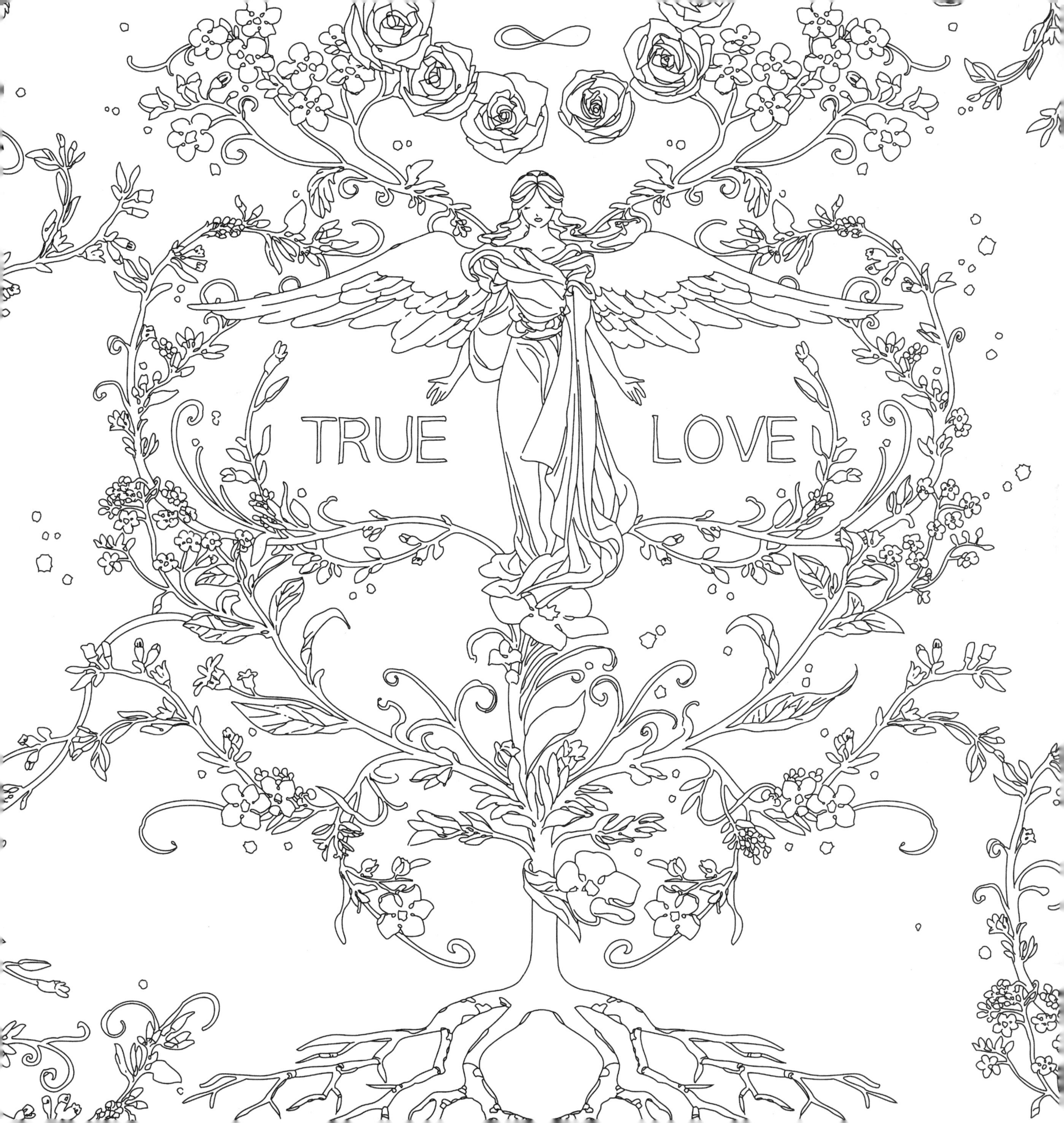
TRUE
LOVE

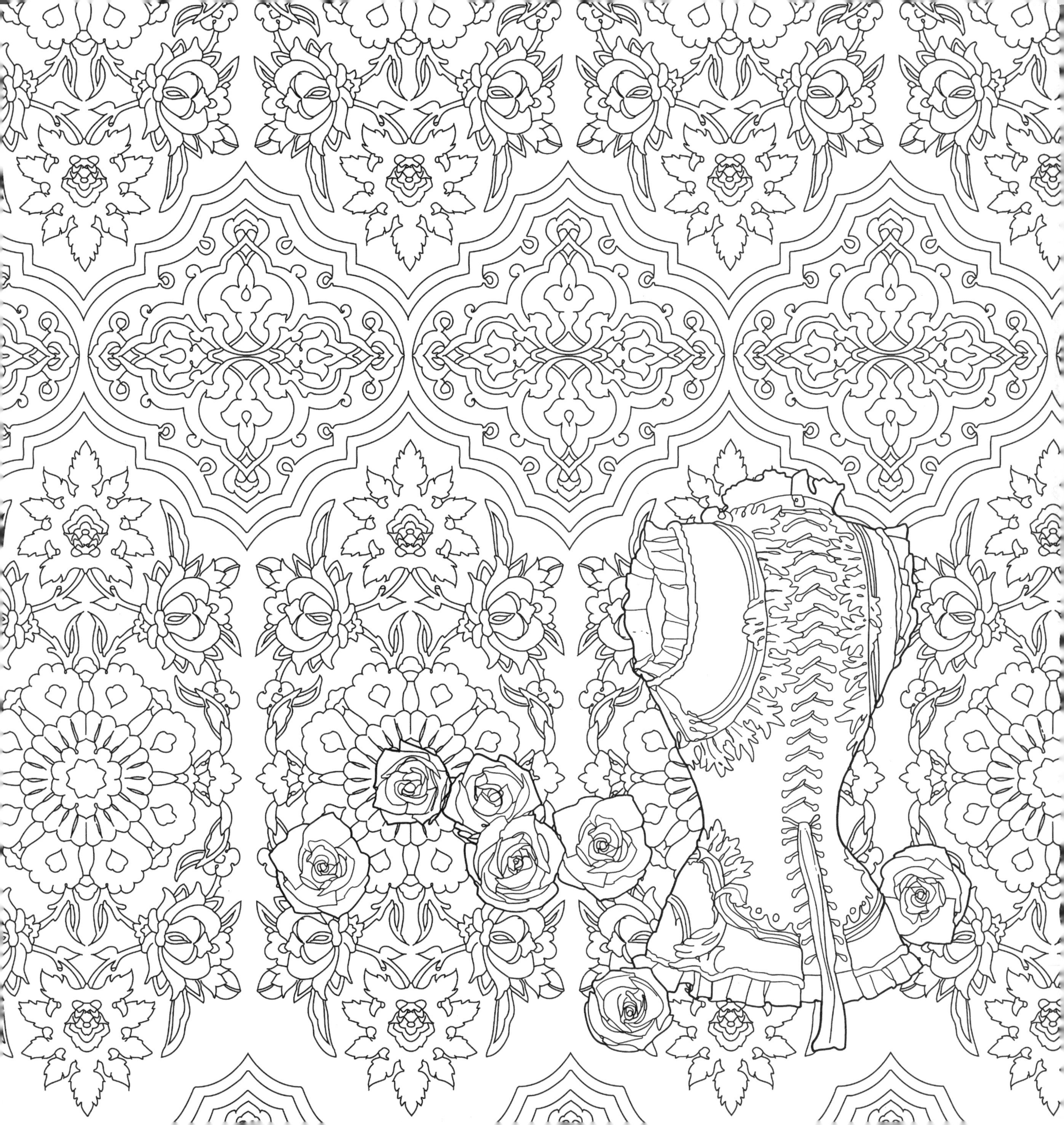

BEAUTY & THE BEAST
Illustration Index

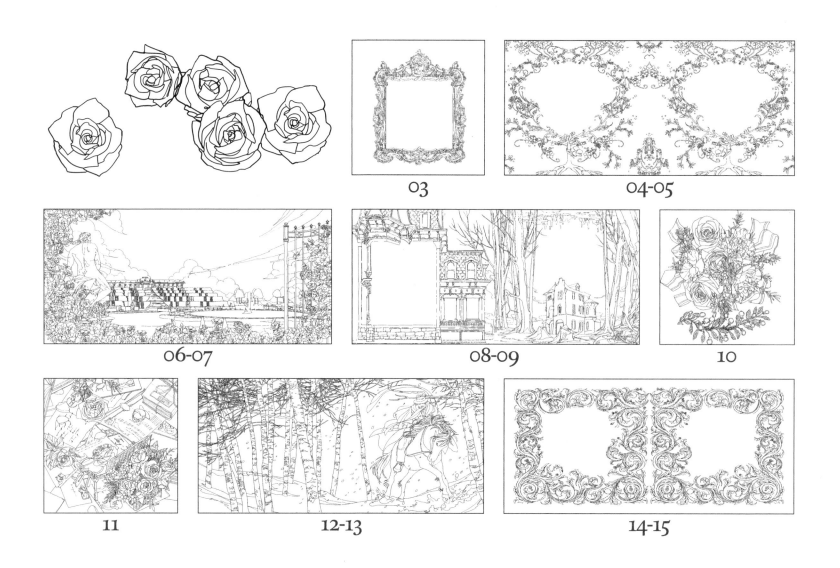

03

04-05

06-07

08-09

10

11

12-13

14-15

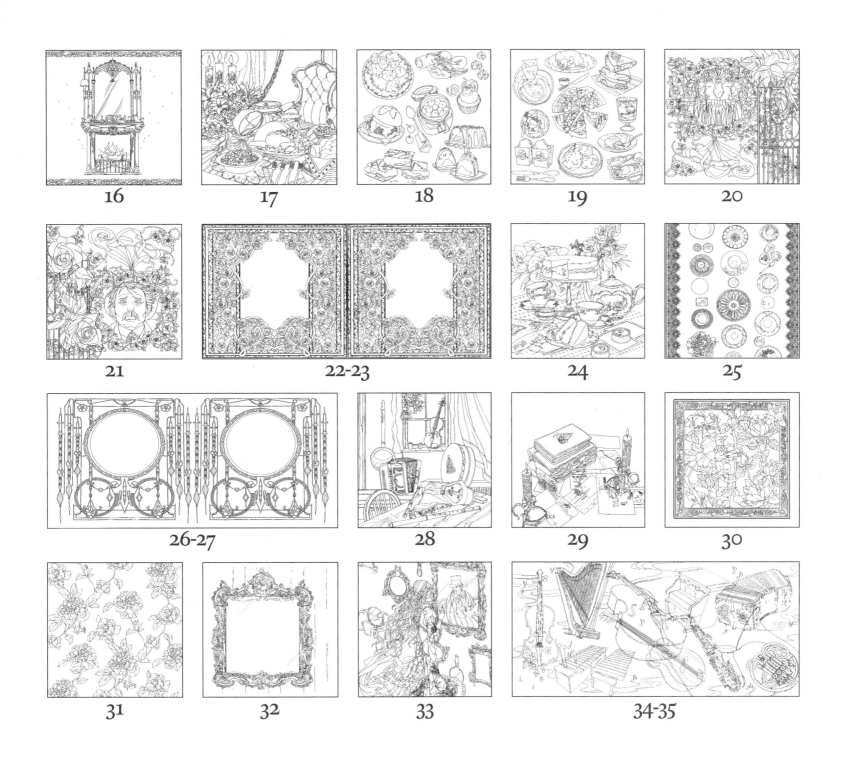

16

17

18

19

20

21

22-23

24

25

26-27

28

29

30

31

32

33

34-35

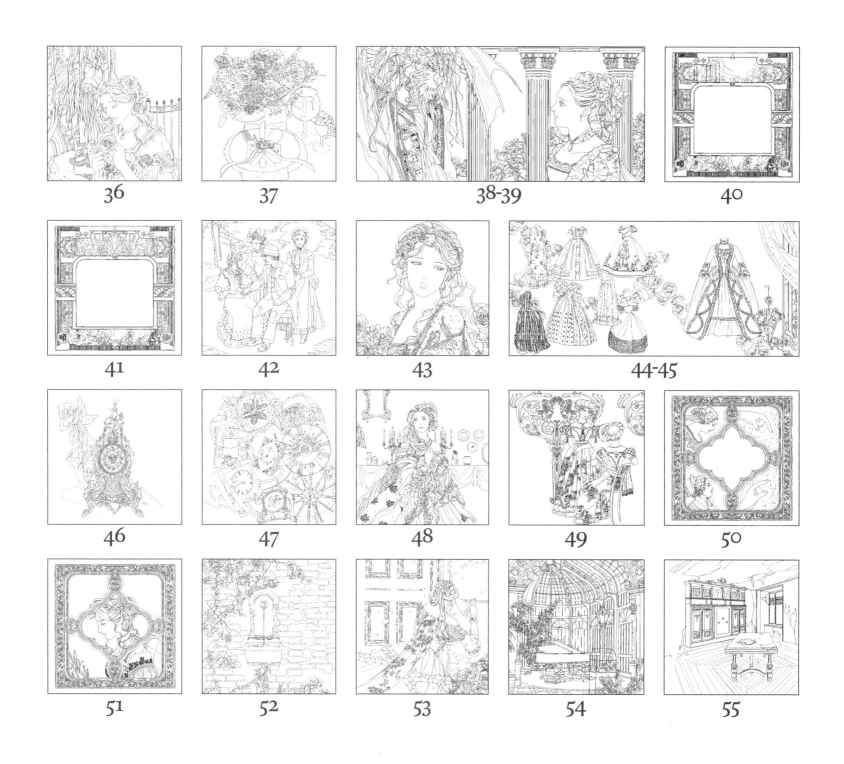

36

37

38-39

40

41

42

43

44-45

46

47

48

49

50

51

52

53

54

55

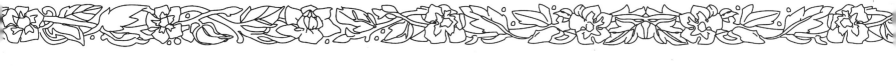

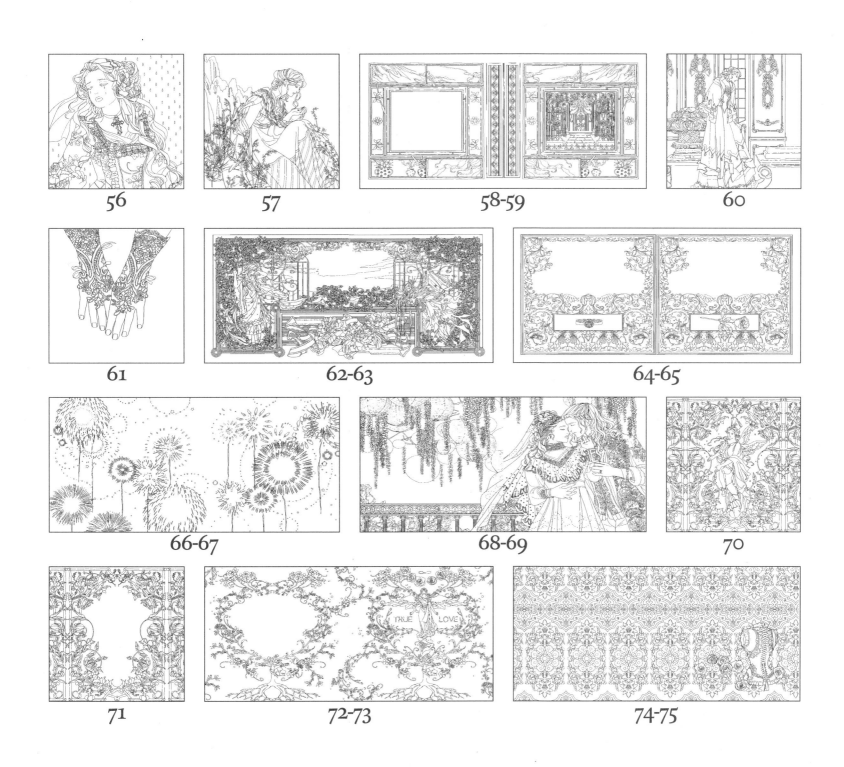

56

57

58-59

60

61

62-63

64-65

66-67

68-69

70

71

TRUE
LOVE
72-73

74-75

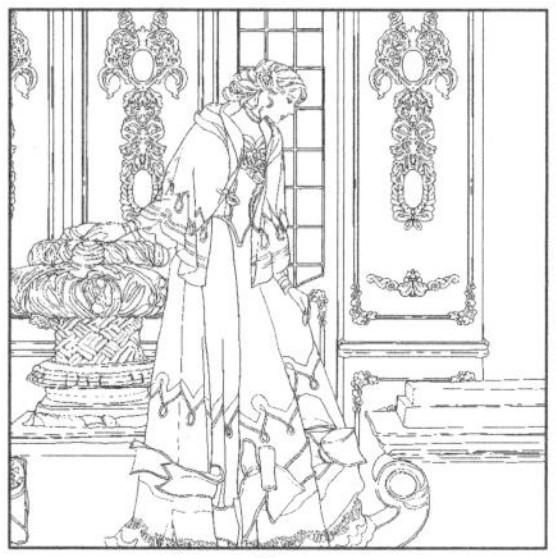

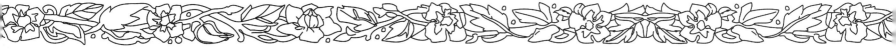